Discover the DARK ENCHANTMENT

Other titles in the **DARK ENCHANTMENT** series

BLOOD DANCE   Louise Cooper
FIRESPELL   Louise Cooper
THE HOUNDS OF WINTER   Louise Cooper
DANCE WITH THE VAMPIRE   J. B. Calchman
HOUSE OF THORNS   Judy Delaghty
KISS OF THE VAMPIRE   J. B. Calchman
THE LOST BRIDES   Theresa Radcliffe
PORTRAIT OF FEAR   Judy Delaghty
VALLEY OF WOLVES   Theresa Radcliffe

The Shrouded Mirror

LOUISE COOPER

D0313683

PUFFIN BOOKS

PUFFIN BOOKS

Published by the Penguin Group
Penguin Books Ltd, 27 Wrights Lane, London w8 5tz, England
Penguin Books USA Inc., 375 Hudson Street, New York,
New York 10014, USA
Penguin Books Australia Ltd, Ringwood, Victoria, Australia
Penguin Books Canada Ltd, 10 Alcorn Avenue, Toronto, Ontario,
Canada m4v 3b2
Penguin Books (NZ) Ltd, 182–190 Wairau Road, Auckland 10,
New Zealand

Penguin Books Ltd, Registered Offices: Harmondsworth, Middlesex,
England

First published 1996
1 3 5 7 9 10 8 6 4 2

Typeset by Datix International Limited, Bungay, Suffolk
Printed in England by Clays Ltd, St Ives plc
Set in 12/14pt Monotype Sabon

CHAPTER I

AS THE CARRIAGE pulled up in the court-yard of the great house, Aline's stomach felt as if it was full of butterflies. She heard the coachman get down, and moments later the carriage door was opened. She stepped out, and saw her new home for the first time.

The house looked daunting. High, grey stone walls towered before her to a roof of gables and tall chimneys, and wide stone steps led up to an imposing front door. Aline clutched her small valise more tightly and tried not to tremble.

She could hardly believe that she was here. Everything had happened so *quickly*. Only a week ago she had been working as a humble helper at the dreary little school in her home village. Then Mrs Rosell had come into her life, and everything had changed.

Mrs Rosell was the housekeeper at a mansion a day's drive away from Aline's village. Her employer, a young man whom she referred to as 'Master Orlando', had asked her to find a girl to become a companion to his sister, who had been injured in an accident and could no longer walk. Someone in the village had recommended Aline, and so Mrs Rosell had come to the school to see her. And to Aline's astonishment, she had offered her the post on the spot.

Aline's parents had been delighted, for this was an undreamed-of chance for their daughter. From a lady's companion, Aline might move on to become a proper teacher one day, or even a governess. It was a step up in the world. So, hardly knowing what to think or what to do, Aline had accepted Mrs Rosell's offer.

Now, though, she felt desperately nervous. What awaited her here? Would she like her new employers and, more importantly, would they like her? And could she, a girl from a poor home, settle happily into life among wealthy strangers?

As the thoughts churned in her mind the front door opened and Mrs Rosell came out. She was a small, plump, comfortable-looking woman, and she greeted Aline with a smile.

'Here you are, my dear! Come in, come in. I'll take you to your room. Hurry, now – Miss Orielle is anxious to meet you.'

Heart thumping and feeling queasy, Aline followed her up the steps and into the entrance hall. She had a bewildering impression of fine tapestries, polished floors and several huge and shining gilt-framed mirrors before Mrs Rosell led her up a wide, sweeping staircase to the upper floor. Then came a maze of corridors, richly carpeted and with more mirrors on the walls, until at last a door was opened and she was shown into the room that would be hers from now on.

Aline stood on the threshold and stared. The room was huge, and beautifully furnished with a fine bed, elegant dressing-table and thick rugs on the floor.

'I've never seen such a lovely room,' she said wonderingly. 'Is it really for me?'

Mrs Rosell smiled. 'All for you, child. It's next door to Miss Orielle's bedroom, so you'll be close by if she needs anything at night.'

Aline went to the window – her feet made no sound on the plush rugs – and looked out. The window gave a view of elegant gardens, with hedges, statues and paved paths meandering between beds filled with spring flowers. To the left was a high hedge with parkland beyond, and to the right –

Aline was suddenly motionless as she saw what lay to the right. Another part of the house . . . but it was a ruin. The windows had no glass, and half the roof had fallen in, leaving rafters gaping starkly to the sky. She could see a huge hole where a chimney-stack had once stood. And the stonework was blackened, as if it had been burned.

'Ah . . . the old north wing.' Mrs Rosell had moved up so quietly that Aline jumped. Aline looked at her, and saw that her eyes were filled with sadness – and also with a hint of bitter anger.

'There was a fire?' she asked softly.

'Yes,' said Mrs Rosell. 'It happened two years

ago. The blaze started in the middle of the night. The whole family slept in that wing then, and by the time the alarm was raised, the fire had too great a hold.' She sighed. 'Master Orlando was so brave. He got Miss Orielle to safety. But the poor master and mistress . . . no one could reach them in time.'

Aline's eyes widened. She had been told that her employers' parents were both dead, but she hadn't dreamed that it had happened in such a terrible way. She said so, and Mrs Rosell replied sombrely, 'Well, now you know the story. And since that night, Miss Orielle has been unable to walk.'

'She was hurt?' Aline asked.

But to her surprise, Mrs Rosell shook her head. 'Not seriously. She was trapped when a beam fell, but by a miracle she suffered no real physical harm. It was the shock of it, that was what the doctors said. They believe she *could* walk again, if only she could find the will. But somehow she can't bring herself even to try.' A sad smile came to her face and she met Aline's gaze. 'Now that you're here, though, who knows whether that might not change? Perhaps all she needs is a friend to help her. That's what Master Orlando hopes.'

Aline felt a prickle of discomfort. Whatever sort of person, she wondered, was Master Orlando expecting her to be? If he thought that she might succeed where all the doctors had failed, then she would surely disappoint him. She was no miracle-worker. She was nothing special at all.

Mrs Rosell, oblivious of Aline's uneasiness, said briskly, 'Now, my dear, you'd better get ready and come downstairs. Tea will be ready in the drawing-room, and Miss Orielle is waiting.'

Aline's nerves gave a sharp little tingle and, mouth dry, she nodded.

'Oh, and one last thing,' added Mrs Rosell. 'Whatever you do, don't mention Miss Orielle's accident in her hearing. Or the fire.' She sighed. 'She and Master Orlando don't like to be reminded of it. That's very important, and you mustn't ever forget.'

'I understand,' Aline said. 'I'll be careful.'

Mrs Rosell gave her directions to the drawing-room, then left her to prepare herself. When she had gone, Aline changed her travelling clothes for a plain but respectable day dress – the best one she had – then sat down before the dressing-table mirror to tidy her hair. Her face, gazing back at her from the glass, looked pinched and a little frightened, and with a great effort she made herself smile and relax. That was better: at least she looked more confident, even if she didn't feel it. After all, she told herself, she had nothing to be afraid of.

She began to brush her hair. It was the colour of corn and, her mother always said, the only thing that prevented her from being plain. Behind her she could see the reflection of the window with its long curtain. Then, as the brush smoothed rhythmically down, the curtain stirred suddenly.

Aline started and swung round. Odd . . . the window wasn't open and there was no draught. And the curtain was motionless now. That glimpse in the mirror must have been her imagination. Silly of her.

With a small shrug, she turned to the glass again and continued with her brushing.

'Miss Orielle,' said Mrs Rosell, 'here is Aline.'

Aline stepped into the elegant drawing-room. In its centre was a big, highly polished table, where fine china and silver were set out ready for tea. Beyond the table were tall windows that let in the afternoon sun. And by one of the windows, someone was sitting in a wheeled chair.

Small white hands reached out and expertly turned the chair around, and Orielle said, 'Aline – welcome to our house.'

Orielle was about the same age as Aline. And she was beautiful, with jet-black hair, porcelain skin and grey eyes that had real warmth in them. There was warmth in her smile, too, and Aline's nerves melted as she went forward to greet her.

'I've so looked forward to your coming,' Orielle said. 'I do hope we'll be the best of friends.'

'I hope so, too,' Aline replied with a smile. 'And . . . thank you for offering me this post.'

'Thank my brother, not me,' Orielle said. 'He made all the arrangements – you'll meet him soon. Mrs Rosell, will you tell Orlando that tea is ready, please?'

'Of course, miss.' Mrs Rosell bustled out, and Orielle wheeled her chair up to the table.

'Come and sit beside me, Aline. You must be hungry after your long journey – if Orlando isn't here in five minutes, we'll start without him.'

Aline looked at the lavish spread. She had never seen anything like it, and suddenly she grew nervous again. Would her manners be good enough for such an elegant household? And as for the china . . . the thought of using such beautiful cups and plates daunted her. What if nervousness made her clumsy and she broke something?

Orielle had begun to talk about the things she wanted to do now that she had a companion. Suddenly the door opened. Aline looked up and saw Orlando for the first time.

He was several years older than his sister. And if Orielle was beautiful, he was without any doubt the most handsome young man Aline had ever set eyes on. His hair, like Orielle's, was as black as ebony; he was tall, slim, and in his finely cut breeches and coat he looked the perfect model of a noble and wealthy young gentleman. And the smile on his lips and in his grey eyes made Aline's heart turn over.

'You must be Aline.' He came forward and

clasped her hand in greeting. 'I'm so glad to meet you – and so glad you were able to accept the post!'

Aline hardly knew what she was saying as she stammered out a reply. She knew she was blushing deeply, but Orlando didn't seem to notice. He went to Orielle's chair and gave her a hug, which she returned with an affectionate kiss. He then took his seat at the table. Orielle was eager to know all that he had been doing that afternoon, and he launched immediately into an account. It was obvious to Aline that he and his sister were very close; far closer than she and her own brothers had ever been. Somehow that reassured her, and gradually she began to recover from her initial confusion. A servant came in with tea, and as the meal progressed she slowly found the confidence to join in the cheerful talk. But she could hardly take her eyes off Orlando. And by the time they had finished eating, her confusion had taken a new turn. She not only found Orlando extremely attractive; she also truly *liked* him. And she had the impression that he liked her, for he behaved towards her with a warmth that seemed just a little greater than mere kindness. He drew her into the conversation, wanted to know about her life and her interests, and once or twice she had caught him looking at her in a strangely thoughtful way. When he saw that she had noticed, he turned his attention back to his meal – but not before giving her a quick, encouraging smile that made her cheeks colour again.

Orielle, however, seemed unaware of Aline's fascination with her brother, and when the dishes had been cleared away she asked to be taken upstairs so that she could show Aline her bedroom. Two servants carried her in her wheelchair, and over her shoulder Orielle joked to Aline, still below in the hall, about the comical sight she must present.

'She's so cheerful,' Aline said softly to Orlando, who had come to stand beside her. 'And yet to be unable to walk . . . it must be very hard for her.'

Orlando smiled a little sadly. 'I think she's grown used to it now.'

'Mrs Rosell said . . .' Aline hesitated, then decided that there was no harm in continuing. 'She said the doctors think there's no real reason why she shouldn't be able to walk.'

'That's true. Her legs are undamaged; in fact she can stand up, if she has something to hold on to. But she can't seem to make herself take that first, vital step.' Orlando looked at Aline, a strange, intense look. 'Perhaps you can help her, Aline. Perhaps you'll be able to give her the confidence she needs. I do hope so.'

Aline didn't answer. If Orlando was looking for a miracle-worker, she thought, then he had made a poor choice. She was no such thing. But she would try. For Orielle's sake – and for his.

'Aline!' Orielle's voice floated down the stairs. 'Come up and see my room!'

Orlando laughed. 'She won't be content until she's shown you all her clothes and had you try half of them on! Goodnight, Aline.' He smiled again, and, although she knew it was silly of her, Aline felt an inward glow of pleasure. 'I'll look forward to seeing you tomorrow.'

CHAPTER II

BY THE TIME she climbed into her new bed that night, Aline was tired, but very happy. The two girls had spent the whole evening in Orielle's room. Overcoming her timidity, Aline had been persuaded to try on many of Orielle's clothes, and Orielle had declared she would see to it that Aline had a new wardrobe of her own. They were getting to know each other quickly. Aline had told Orielle about her home and family, and Orielle in turn talked about her love of flowers and music and reading, and of the new pony and trap in which she wanted to go driving as soon as the weather was warm enough. She also talked a great deal about Orlando. She was clearly very proud of him, and of the way he had taken so much on his shoulders since their parents died. He ran the estate, looked after their father's business, and also cared devotedly for her, which was another great responsibility. But then, Orielle added fondly, she and Orlando had always been very close, and he had always done all he could for her.

She said nothing else about her parents, and nothing at all about the tragedy which had killed them and paralysed her. Aline would have liked to find out more but, remembering Mrs Rosell's warning, she hadn't asked any questions. Now though, as she snuffed out her candle, she couldn't help thinking about the terrible fire. Why, she wondered, hadn't the gutted north wing been rebuilt? Not for lack of money, that was certain. Orlando and Orielle were wealthy – and besides, to see the wing standing there stark and grim must be a constant and hideous reminder to them. Surely it would be better even to demolish it, than do nothing?

Aline yawned. The puzzle of the north wing was not her concern, and she felt too tired to think about it any more. Moonlight was filtering in through the window; she could see it reflected in the glass of her dressing-table mirror. Despite the strangeness of her surroundings, she told herself, she would sleep well tonight.

But she didn't sleep well. Instead, her night was filled with strange, vague dreams, and at last she woke with a start to find herself staring into the darkness of the unfamiliar room. Everything was very still, and for a few moments she lay quietly, wondering what had disturbed her.

Then, soft in the dark, she heard a sound.

Aline tensed. Was she imagining it? She couldn't be sure, for the sound was so quiet and steady that it was hard to pinpoint. Possibly it was just the night breeze rustling . . . and yet it seemed to be *in* the room, not outside. As if the curtain was stirring, and brushing against the floor.

Or as if someone was breathing very close by . . .

Aline's skin began to crawl, and her voice broke from her throat in a nervous squeak. '*Who is it?*' she quavered. '*Is someone there?*'

Instantly the sound stopped. The room was utterly silent. Heart pounding, Aline counted to twenty before she dared move – then, quickly, she reached for the candle beside her bed and lit it.

The candlelight cast menacing shadows on the walls, but they *were* only shadows. Aline gazed fearfully around, then at last let out her breath in a sigh. No one had crept in; no one was there. Those sounds must have been the breeze after all – or even just an echo of her dreams. She had let her imagination run away with her.

Chiding herself for being so silly, Aline snuggled deeper into her blankets. Best to go back to sleep. Morning would come soon, and there was nothing to be afraid of.

Orielle was up early, and as she was carried downstairs she asked Aline if she had slept well. Aline almost told her about the eerie incident in the night, but then changed her mind. Orielle was just being polite – and anyway, the whole thing had been nonsense. So she simply said yes, thank you, and turned her attention to the excitement of her first full day at the house.

The girls had breakfast together, and afterwards, as the weather was fine, Orielle wanted to show Aline the gardens. So Aline spent the morning pushing the wheelchair along paths and across terraces and around mazes. Before long Orlando came to join them. Orielle was delighted to see him, and as Aline greeted him her heart gave a little lurch. She felt dismayed – surely she wasn't starting to have romantic feelings for Orlando? The idea was ridiculous. He was her employer and couldn't possibly have any other interest in her, and if she started entertaining any other notions then she would only hurt herself and spoil her future here. Orlando was kind. He was attractive. He was willing to be her friend. But that was all, and she must not allow herself to be foolish.

The tour of the garden continued. They visited all of Orlando's and Orielle's favourite spots, from the ornamental pool with its fish and fountains to the rose-bower by a mellow old wall, and as she listened to their nostalgic stories about this place or that, Aline felt wistfully envious of their closeness and the memories they so fondly shared. She felt like an intruder in their private world, and wondered if she should go back to the house and leave them alone. But when she suggested it, Orlando insisted that she must stay. In fact, he said, he was tired of walking sedately – he had a much better idea.

'I challenge you.' He grinned. 'Let's see who

can push Orielle's chair faster along one of the straight paths!'

It was a frivolous, hilarious race, and it restored Aline's spirits — which was exactly what Orlando had intended. Orielle shrieked with excitement as the chair bucketed along faster, and Orlando gallantly declared Aline the winner. When the bell rang for lunch they all went indoors dishevelled and breathless. Mrs Rosell nodded approval at the colour that had come to Orielle's pale cheeks.

'You're doing her a world of good already,' she told Aline. 'And Master Orlando thinks so, too. That smile of his . . . it's just like the old days!'

Startled, Aline glanced at Orlando. He *did* look happy, and as she watched him he suddenly caught her eye and his smile took on a new warmth. Aline felt herself blushing. Hoping that no one had noticed her reaction, she quickly looked away.

Days went by, and as Aline and Orielle got to know each other better they soon became close. From the beginning Orielle treated Aline as a friend rather than a servant, and the two girls spent a great deal of time together, out of doors when the weather allowed or in the house talking or playing games when it did not. Aline was learning a great many things which she had never dreamed of in the past; from picking out tunes on the spinet (which Orielle could play beautifully) to driving Orielle's little pony-chaise in the park that surrounded the house. Orielle had ordered two new dresses to be made for Aline, and she had a new cloak, new hat and even fine new shoes and slippers. Sometimes Aline had to stop and pinch herself to be sure that her life at the great house wasn't a dream from which she would suddenly wake.

But there was one cloud on her horizon, and that was the problem of Orlando. For, however hard she tried, she couldn't stem her secret yearnings for him. Over and over again she told herself that she was just infatuated, and even if it was more than that, nothing could possibly come of it for their worlds were too far apart. But while her head said one thing, her heart was starting to say another, and all the logic in the world couldn't stop it. She was falling in love with Orlando.

Aline did her best to hide her feelings, but it was far from easy. And as the days passed, Orlando's attitude towards her started to make matters worse – for he was showing greater and greater interest in her.

At first she didn't think that there was anything unusual in the amount of time that Orlando spent with her and Orielle. She thought it was simply that he enjoyed his sister's company, and only when Orielle remarked that she was seeing much more of him than she had before Aline arrived did Aline wonder if there was more to it.

She began to notice the way Orlando looked at her. She began to notice how often he addressed remarks to her rather than to Orielle. And, though she could barely believe it, she began to suspect that he might feel more than friendship towards her.

Orielle, too, had seen the change in her brother, and Aline knew she was uneasy about it. Presumably Orielle thought that a near-servant was not good enough for him. Aline didn't know what to do. She had grown very fond of Orielle and didn't want to upset her; and she was also very afraid of coming between brother and sister. But every day her feelings for Orlando grew stronger. If she wasn't to ruin everything she had here, she must hide her emotions.

Though it hurt her to do it, Aline forced herself to be cool and distant towards Orlando, hoping that he would be put off. Another week went by, and she thought that the ploy was working. But then, one rainy afternoon when Orielle had been carried upstairs to rest, Orlando found Aline alone in the drawing-room.

He came in, pushing the door behind him. 'Aline,' he said, 'I want to talk to you.'

Aline tensed, and forced herself to smile. 'Is it about Orielle?'

'No,' Orlando replied. 'It's about us. You and me.'

Aline stared uneasily at him. 'I . . . don't know what you mean.'

'I think you do.' He came towards her. She didn't back away, but her heart began to pound. Then his hands came to rest on her shoulders, and a tingling sensation went through her.

'Orlando, please don't!' she said in distress.

'Why not?'

'Because . . .' Her voice wavered, and suddenly all the sensible reasons why he shouldn't meant nothing. She turned her head away, unable to speak.

'Aline, look at me.' Gently Orlando turned her to face him again. His expression was very serious. 'Look into my eyes and tell me, if you can, that you don't feel anything for me.'

Aline tried to say the words he challenged her to say. But it was impossible. She felt tears spring to her eyes, and instead heard herself whisper, 'I can't . . .'

For perhaps five seconds Orlando continued to gaze at her. Then, very gently but very deliberately, he leaned towards her and kissed her. For an instant Aline tensed as though about to pull away . . . then suddenly the barriers she had built collapsed. She returned his kiss with all the longing and passion she had suppressed, and for what seemed an endless time they clung together.

At last they broke apart. Quietly, Orlando said, 'I've wanted to kiss you for such a long time.'

Aline was close to tears. 'I wish you hadn't . . .' she whispered.

'Why? You care for me, even if you've tried to pretend you don't. I've seen it in your face, Aline. And you must have realized that I feel the same. Why have you tried to keep me at bay?'

Aline tried to speak but couldn't, then suddenly she broke down and all the doubts she had harboured came tumbling out. It wasn't *right* for them to love each other. They were from different worlds. She wasn't rich. His family and friends would say she wasn't good enough.

'That's not true!' Orlando protested fiercely. 'What sort of person do you think I am? I don't care where you come from, or if your family has money. Those things don't matter – it's *you* I love.'

'But they *do* matter,' Aline argued. 'Even if you don't care about them, other people do.'

'What other people?'

She hadn't wanted to say it, but . . . 'Orielle, for one,' she told him sadly. 'I'm sure she's guessed, Orlando. And she doesn't like it.'

To her astonishment, Orlando laughed incredulously. 'Orielle?' he echoed. 'She's the very *last* person to think such a thing! Oh, Aline, is that what's worrying you – that Orielle won't approve? You're wrong. She'll be happy for us both.'

Aline tried to protest, tried to tell him about the uneasiness that she had sensed in Orielle. But Orlando wouldn't listen. She had admitted she loved him, and couldn't pretend any more.

'Don't worry about Orielle,' Orlando told her gently. 'I'll tell her the truth, and –'

'No!' Aline caught hold of his arm. 'No, Orlando, please don't. At least, not yet.' She swallowed. 'Maybe I *am* being silly, but . . . let's say nothing to her – or to anyone – for a while longer. Just until I feel a little more secure.'

'But you *are* secure! Don't you believe that?'

She wanted to believe it; wanted to with all her heart. But the memory of how Orielle sometimes looked at them when they were together made her feel uneasy.

'Please,' she said again. 'For me, Orlando. If you really do care, then say nothing to Orielle. Just for a little while.'

Orlando took her face between his hands and smiled at her. 'All right. If it makes you happy, I promise it.' He kissed her again. 'But I won't be able to keep our secret for *too* long!'

Aline pushed a loose strand of hair behind her ear. 'I'd better go,' she said, fumbling for an excuse to get away, to be alone, to *think*. 'Orielle will be bored with resting, and I promised to teach her a new card game . . .'

She almost ran from the room, leaving him gazing after her. The door was half open; she slipped through . . .

And saw Orielle.

She was wheeling herself across the hall, and as she heard Aline's footsteps she turned and looked at her. Aline knew immediately that she had overheard the conversation in the drawing-room. And for one moment, before she could mask it with a cheerful smile, she saw a strange and – there was no other word for it – *haunted* look in Orielle's eyes.

CHAPTER III

THAT NIGHT, ALINE dreamed about the north wing.

It had happened on one or two nights before, but this time the dream was much more vivid and unpleasant. She woke from it with a start and jerked bolt upright in bed, heart thundering and breath catching in her throat.

Smoke and darkness and a sense of hideous oppression ... Aline shuddered, pushing the memory of the dream away, and reached out to reassure herself that the candle she had left beside her bed was still there. Her fingers touched the brass candlestick – and three clear words whispered through the room.

'*I hate you.*'

Aline felt as if she had turned to stone. Eyes widening, she stared into the darkness. But her curtains were closed tightly tonight, shutting out the moonlight, and she could see nothing, not even the dim outlines of furniture.

'*I hate you. I hate you.*'

It was coming from within the room. It was only a few steps away from her bed ... A thick, suffocating sense of terror began to rise in Aline and she couldn't crush it. Someone was here. Someone was in the room with her . . .

'*I hate you, I hate you, I hate you . . .*' It was a girl's voice, only a whisper, but there was fury in it, fury and loathing and cruelty. Aline's nerve snapped, and with a sound that was half gasp and half shout she snatched at the candlestick. She missed; the candlestick crashed from the table and on to the floor, and in terror Aline flung herself sideways, half out of bed, groping for it, desperate, wanting *light* –

But then she grew still as she realized that the whispering had stopped.

She found the candlestick. Her fingers clenched tightly round it and, very slowly, she raised her head and stared again into the dark. There was no sound. No sense of anyone moving.

Aline scrabbled to light the candle, and as the flame caught she held it high, pushing back the darkness.

As before, on her first night in the house, there was no one there. Her door was closed. All seemed well.

But this time, Aline couldn't convince herself that it had been a dream.

Her heart was still thumping like a hammer against her ribs and she took several deep breaths in an effort to calm herself. Then, still holding the candle, she climbed out of bed and padded cautiously across the room. Yes, the door definitely was closed. But the handle turned easily

and silently, and the hinges didn't squeak. Someone *could* have crept in without waking her. And
they could also have hurried out again while she
was fumbling for the lost candlestick.

With a quick movement Aline pulled the door
open and looked out on to the landing. It was
empty. Everything was still. Then she glanced at
Orielle's bedroom door. If someone *had* been
prowling, might they have disturbed Orielle, and
could she too have heard something?

Aline tiptoed to Orielle's door, eased it open a
little and looked in. By the glow from her candle
she could just make out a dim, humped shape in
the bed. Orielle was still asleep. With a sigh Aline
closed the door again and turned to go back to
her own room.

Then abruptly a flicker of movement caught
her eye. Aline spun round, and glimpsed a vague
shape at the end of the passage. It was dressed in
something long and white and filmy, and as she
moved she was just in time to see it dart across
the landing and vanish.

Aline dropped the candlestick. It bounced, the
candle went out and the landing was plunged
into moon-shot darkness. Horrified, she clutched
at the wall . . . then the momentary panic passed
as logic came to her rescue. That figure hadn't
just disappeared into thin air. There was a side
corridor at the end of the landing; it led to the
back staircase and from there to the kitchen.
What had happened just now was no dream and

no hallucination – someone was playing a cruel joke on her!

Anger eclipsed her fear, and she started to run down the landing in pursuit of the pale shape. With luck she would catch whoever it was on the stairs, and then –

The thought broke off in a surge of terror as, with no warning, a white, fluttering form launched itself at her out of the dark. With a cry of stark fear Aline recoiled; her foot caught in the hem of her nightgown, she lost her balance and fell to the floor.

Then, as she pulled herself dizzily on to hands and knees, she realized her mistake. There was a long mirror on the wall at the end of the landing. She had been running towards it, and as she neared it, an image of herself had seemed to rush out of the glass. There was no white horror to menace her. It had been nothing more than her own reflection.

Aline felt utterly foolish. Not only had she been terrified by her own mirror image but, she realized now, the first pale figure hadn't really been there at all. Again, she had merely glimpsed herself in the glass and had jumped to the conclusion that someone was prowling about the house. What an idiot she was! She had had a nightmare, that was all. There had been no whispering voice, and no one in her room. She had risked waking half the household, and all for nothing.

Thankfully, though, it seemed that no one else had woken, and so, feeling abashed, Aline returned to her own room. She didn't bother to light the candle again; instead she pulled the curtains back a little way, allowing the moonlight to slant in. Slipping under the blankets, she was soon asleep.

And so she knew nothing of what took place a few minutes later. She did not see the faint, chilly light – not moonlight but something else – that seeped into her room, glowing under her door from the passage outside. The light hovered for a few moments, then slowly faded away. And as it vanished, there was a small, soft noise. Like the rustle of a skirt . . . or someone breathing.

Aline soon forgot the strange incident and settled back to the comfortable and ordinary routine of everyday life. And in the wake of the emotional confrontation with Orlando she had a new and precious secret to keep.

They snatched a little time alone whenever they could, sometimes walking in the park beyond the house or sometimes sitting up late in the drawing-room after Orielle had gone to bed. Orlando had kept his promise and said nothing to Orielle about their love for each other, but, as he wryly admitted to Aline, that was growing harder and harder to do.

'Orielle must know how we both feel,' he said, taking Aline's hands in his and kissing them.

'And you *are* wrong to think that she won't approve. I know she will.'

Aline was still unsure. But over the next few days Orlando persisted, and at last he made a plea to her that she couldn't refuse.

'It's my birthday soon,' he said, one morning over an early breakfast while Orielle was still upstairs. 'And I'm planning to hold a ball here in the house. All our neighbours and friends will come. But I want you and no one else to be my dancing partner. And when the ball is at its height, I mean to announce our betrothal!'

Aline stared at him, stunned. 'Our . . . *betrothal*?' She hadn't dreamed that this would happen; though she knew Orlando loved her, she hadn't *dared* to dream it.

But then on the heels of her joy came dismay. 'Orlando, you can't!' she protested.

'Oh, but I can. And I will.' Orlando smiled at her. 'I'm sorry, Aline, I just can't keep the secret any longer. I want you to be my wife, and I want the world to know it.'

Aline tried to argue, but this time Orlando was determined. They would tell Orielle the truth this very morning, he declared. Aline would see for herself how pleased she was, and that would put paid to her fears once and for all. At last Aline gave way. She couldn't sway him . . . and in her heart she wanted this as much as he did. If Orielle did approve, as he promised, it would set a crown on her happiness and make it perfect.

They broke their news to Orielle later that morning. And as Orlando spoke the words, Aline knew instantly that something was very wrong. Orielle's face froze, and a look of shock – almost of horror – came into her eyes. In a small, stunned voice she said, 'Betrothed . . .?'

'Isn't it wonderful?' Orlando must have seen his sister's disquiet, but he ignored it. Then, with a tremendous effort, Orielle snapped out of her paralysis. A shiver went through her – Aline saw it clearly – and her face and voice changed. 'Oh . . .' she said. 'Oh, yes . . . it *is* wonderful. I'm so thrilled for you both!' She reached up to hug and kiss Aline, adding, 'Dear Aline – now I shall have a sister as well as a brother.'

Aline returned the kiss, trying to convince herself that Orielle's first reaction had been no more than momentary surprise. Orlando seemed untroubled by it, and he knew his sister far better than she did. Now Orielle was congratulating them both, asking eagerly about the ball; behaving, in fact, as if she was as happy as they were. Yet there still seemed to be something brittle in her manner. Something that didn't quite ring true.

Orlando had begun to tell Orielle about his plans for the ball. Aline must have a new gown, of course; and as she had never learned to dance, some lessons must be arranged. Suddenly, and to Aline's surprise, Orielle launched enthusiastically into the discussion. She would take care of everything, she said. She would oversee the making of the gown, and as for dancing – well, even if she could no longer dance, she could teach Aline all the proper steps, and it would be the next best thing to taking the floor herself. Listening to her, Aline's fears started to fade. Orielle seemed genuinely happy now, and ready to help in any way that she could. In fact she was eager to be involved in every aspect of Aline's preparations, as though she was actually proud of her.

'I'll lend you jewellery and shoes,' she was saying. 'Of course you'll have your own jewellery soon – I'm sure Orlando will see to that! – but for now I have some things that will suit you perfectly. You'll look beautiful at the ball, Aline. As fine as any great lady.'

The last of Aline's doubts melted away. She had been mistaken – Orielle was not upset or angry; far from disapproving of the betrothal, she was delighted. And that was a tremendous relief, for Aline would have hated anything, even Orlando, to come between them. Orielle was a true friend, and true friends were rare and precious.

CHAPTER IV

ALINE WENT TO bed that night feeling exhilarated. Sitting before her looking-glass and brushing her hair, her mind whirled with thoughts of gowns, jewels and dances, and with joyful daydreams of what the future promised. Her hair glinted in the candle-light. It looked like spun gold tonight. At the ball, she told herself, she would wear it –

The thought collapsed as, from behind her, came a soft, cruel laugh.

Aline's hand stopped rigid in mid-movement and she spun round on the stool. The candle flame fluttered as she turned, and shadows cavorted on the walls . . . but there was no one there. Aline's heart was thumping; she swallowed. Imagining things again . . . with a little shiver she turned back to the mirror.

And for one moment it seemed that the face looking back at her was not her own.

Aline jumped like a startled cat, shaking her head violently. The illusion vanished and her own familiar features returned. It was only a trick of the light, but it had shaken her badly. What was the *matter* with her? Hearing whisperings in the night, seeing things that weren't there in her mirror ... was she going mad?

Or, said a still, small voice inside her, *is someone trying to make you think you are?*

Aline put down her hairbrush and slowly stood up as a terrible thought occurred to her. She had told herself that she had dreamed these eerie incidents. But she wasn't dreaming now. She was wide awake. And that cruel laugh had sounded very, very real.

Was someone in the house trying to frighten her? Had they sneaked into her room while she was sleeping, and were the things she had heard more than mere imagination? Her heart was pounding again, and she moved quietly across the floor to get into bed. There was only one way to solve this mystery, she thought. If she did have an unknown enemy, it was likely that whoever it was would strike again tonight. So she must stay awake, listen and watch. If someone came prowling, she would find out the truth.

For more than an hour Aline lay waiting. She would have liked to read, but candlelight might deter her enemy and so she simply stared watchfully into the dark. She was very tired and it was an effort to stay awake; despite her determination her eyes kept closing, and at last she started to drift towards sleep – until, suddenly, something jolted her out of her doze.

The breathing sound had begun again.

Aline's eyes flicked open and her pulse seemed

to stop. Yes; she could hear it clearly. Regular, rhythmic, very soft. Someone was here . . .

Moving with great caution, she sat up. The breathing continued, and as her eyes adjusted to the dimness Aline peered around the room. There was no moon tonight but the stars were out and their faint radiance filtered in through a gap in the curtains. And by that feeble glow she saw a shadow move.

Suddenly the breathing changed. It seemed to distort, like something heard in a feverish nightmare, and the sound of it twisted and became a word, sibilantly and horribly repeated.

'*Hate . . . hate . . . hate . . .*'

Aline's heart missed a beat painfully and she hissed, 'Who's there? Who are you?'

Her challenge fell away into absolute silence. For several seconds there was no sound, no movement; nothing at all. Then out of the dark came a contemptuous giggle.

A shuddering chill went through Aline. *She had heard that laughter before!* Struggling to stay calm she drew breath to call out again – but before she could speak, a mocking little voice whispered through the room.

'*Come and find me, Aline. Come and find my secret . . . if you can!*'

Fear and fury erupted together in Aline's mind and she made a grab for the candle, fumbling to light it and see the intruder. The flame caught, flared – but suddenly a gust from the window whisked through the room, almost snuffing the candle out again. And in the wake of the draught, Aline heard the door bang shut.

The flame steadied and brightened. The room was empty; Aline was alone. But as she stared at the door, suspicion began to crawl in her mind. Perhaps she hadn't closed it properly, and the gust of wind had slammed it. Or perhaps, as she lit the candle, *someone* had run out of her bedroom and into the corridor . . .

She started to slip out of bed. As her foot touched the floor, she heard the unpleasant little giggle again, from the other side of the door.

Aline sprang from the bed and, snatching up her candle, ran to wrench the door open. Holding the light high, she looked out.

The passage was deserted. Aline stared in both directions, even – irrationally – looking upwards, as if her unknown tormentor might have climbed the wall and be clinging to the ceiling. But there was only the empty corridor with its old pictures and furniture, looking gloomy and dreamlike and more than a little menacing in the darkness. Aline shivered, started to withdraw . . .

And froze as a whisper drifted from the end of the passage.

'*Find me if you can . . . find me if you can . . .*'

A tingle of shock coursed through Aline. Too angry to be afraid, she started to run along the corridor in the direction from which the whisper had come. Ahead of her was the long mirror; she saw her own reflection looming in it, started to turn aside — then paused as a strange, intuitive feeling washed over her. Her quarry was very close by. She *knew* it, almost as if the mirror had shown her. Yet when she looked again, she could see only her own figure in the glass.

'Ali-ine . . . *Find me, Aline . . . If you can . . .*'

It came from the side passage that led to the back stairs. Candle flickering, feet stumbling, Aline started to run again, and a weird and almost unearthly hunt began through the rooms and corridors of the old house. The voice kept calling to her, teasing, still giggling; but though she ran this way and that, the mocking taunts were always just ahead of her, just out of reach. And the mirrors added to her confusion. The house had so many of them; time after time she thought she glimpsed someone moving and ran towards them, only to find that it was nothing more than her own image reflected in yet another glass.

But each time that happened, again she couldn't shake off the uneasy feeling that whoever bedevilled her was very close by . . .

Suddenly she found herself in an unfamiliar part of the house. This was another corridor but, unlike all the others, there were no furnishings here. Ahead of her was a single door, shut and peculiarly discoloured; almost as if it had been charred. Everything was very quiet and still, touched with a sense of desolation. And a cold feeling went through Aline as she realized where she was. She had come upon the entrance to the old north wing – the scene of the fatal fire.

Mrs Rosell's warning about the dangers of the north wing echoed in Aline's mind. She took a step back, knowing she should not venture any further.

And from behind the charred door came a soft, malicious laugh.

'*You'll never know my secret, Aline.*' The voice seemed to hiss in the air around her, echoing malevolently. Then it swelled, growing suddenly, shockingly louder. '*And you'll never have Orlando. Never . . . Never . . . NEVER!*'

Aline gave a wild cry and launched herself at the forbidden door. She crashed against it; for a moment it resisted and then the catch gave way. The door flew open, smacking back on its hinges – and out of the blackness beyond, something huge and dark came toppling towards Aline. She heard herself scream in terror and disbelief – it was a mirror, a gigantic mirror with a gilt frame, and out of the mirror a figure was lunging towards her. She had a frantic, momentary impression of flying hair the colour of flame, a twisted face, hands like claws that clutched something sharp and glittering –

The mirror crashed down on her, and she woke with a shout in her own bed.

Eyes wide with shock, Aline sat bolt upright and stared into the cold light of early dawn. A nightmare – it had all been a nightmare! She must have fallen asleep without realizing it, and her hectic imagination had conjured the dream and made her believe it was real. She could have wept with sheer relief, and as her racing pulse started to slow down she pushed a hand under her pillow to find her handkerchief.

A sharp, stabbing pain went through her, and with a gasp of surprise she pulled her hand back. Her finger was bleeding. Something had *cut* her . . . Baffled, Aline sucked at the wound, then pulled the pillow aside to see what had caused it.

On the mattress, under the pillow, lay a long, jagged piece of glass. Aline stared in astonishment, then carefully picked it up. A drop of blood gleamed scarlet on it, and its surface showed a broken reflection of her own horrified face.

Aline began to feel sick. An awful sense of premonition was rising inside her, and with a hand that was suddenly unsteady she turned the glass over.

The other side was covered by a silver backing. It was a piece from a broken mirror.

CHAPTER V

ALINE KNEW NOW that she was in real danger. The eerie night hunt through the house might have been nothing more than a dream, but this new threat was another matter. Someone was trying to frighten her, and possibly they meant to do worse than that. The jagged glass might only be a beginning.

She bandaged her finger – luckily the cut wasn't very deep – then she thought hard about the mystery. Who might her unknown attacker be? Not one of the servants, she was sure, for they were all much older than she was, and the taunting, mocking voice belonged to someone of her own age.

And then with a slow, crawling sense of dread Aline made herself face the one possibility that she had been trying to ignore.

Orielle. On the surface it was ridiculous, for how could a girl in a wheelchair prowl the house as quietly and quickly as her mysterious enemy did? But then again, there was nothing physically wrong with Orielle. In theory, the doctors said, she *could* learn to walk again . . .

Aline stared at the wall that divided her room from Orielle's. Such a short distance. So easy to creep in and then return before anyone could see her. Aline didn't want to believe it, but the clues were starting to add up to an awful suspicion.

Yet what could she do? Certainly not march into Orielle's room and confront her. She had no proof of anything, and if she was wrong, to accuse Orielle would bring disaster on her own head. But how else could she find out the truth?

Aline decided to say nothing to Orielle – but from now on she would watch her very carefully. If Orielle was behind this, then *somehow* Aline would find a way to unmask her.

She got dressed, then put the piece of broken glass carefully away in a drawer and went to Orielle's room. Orielle was awake, and as soon as she saw Aline's face her eyes narrowed.

'Aline?' she said. 'Is something wrong?'

Aline made herself smile. 'No,' she replied. 'I had a bad dream last night and it's left me feeling tired, that's all.'

Orielle tensed visibly. 'A bad dream? What about?'

'Oh . . . just about an empty passage and a strange door.' Aline shrugged, pretending indifference but studying Orielle closely. 'It was nothing really; silly of me to be frightened by it.'

Orielle didn't speak for a few moments. Then: 'What have you done to your hand?'

'This?' Aline glanced casually at the bandage. 'Just an accident. It's only a little cut.' And though Orielle pressed her she wouldn't say any more but changed the subject quickly.

Orielle was very quiet as Aline helped her to dress. She seemed preoccupied, and several times Aline caught her watching covertly, though Orielle turned her head away quickly before their eyes could meet. Aline pretended to notice nothing odd, and soon the servants came to carry Orielle and her chair down to breakfast.

At breakfast Orielle hardly had a word to say. Orlando, puzzled by her silence, tried to cheer her but his efforts failed. Then, when the meal was over and the dishes were being cleared away, Orielle asked him if he would take her out into the garden for a few minutes. She obviously wanted to speak to him alone, and Aline made an excuse and left them. From an adjoining room she heard the wheelchair being pushed across the hall; quickly she went to the window, and a minute later Orlando and Orielle appeared on the terrace. Aline knew that she shouldn't eavesdrop – but this was too important for scruples. Heart quickening, she followed them outside.

They were by the terrace wall, Orielle in her chair while Orlando sat on the balustrade. They both had their backs to Aline, so she was able to hide behind a large ornamental shrub and overhear them.

'. . . she wouldn't tell me what the dream was about,' Orielle was saying. Her voice was unsteady, nervous. 'But I know she dreamed about the north wing, Orlando. I just *know* she did! And her finger's bandaged. Did you see? She cut it – or *something* did.' She drew a deep breath. 'Orlando, you've got to stop this! Stop it, before it gets any worse.'

'Orielle, *you're* the one who's got to stop it!' Orlando replied. He sounded upset. 'You're being ridiculous, making shadows out of nothing.'

'I'm not!' Orielle protested. 'I'm not imagining things, truly I'm not! Aline is in danger, and –'

'She's not in danger. If she was, don't you think I'd know it better than you?' Now Orlando was becoming angry. 'What's the matter with you, Orielle? Don't you want me to be happy?'

'Of course I do, and I want Aline to be happy, too! But if –'

To Aline's frustration – she would have given a great deal to know what Orielle had been about to say – Orlando interrupted again. 'I've had enough of this,' he said. 'You *are* letting your imagination run away with you, and I simply won't listen to any more of it. I'm not going to let anything spoil the love I've found, so let's have an end to this nonsense.' Then, more gently, he added, 'There's nothing to be afraid of; truly there isn't. No one's going to hurt Aline or me. Not now.'

Not now? Whatever did *that* mean? Aline

wondered. Orlando and Orielle had fallen silent, then abruptly, and in a small, weary voice, Orielle said, 'Take me indoors, please, Orlando. There's nothing else I can say.'

Quickly, before they could turn round and see her, Aline slipped from her hiding place and hurried back into the house. She went to her room, and there she sat down to think about what she had overheard.

It seemed that, unless Orielle was very clever indeed, she had been quite wrong to suspect her of treachery. That was a great relief, but it posed new questions which Aline couldn't even begin to answer. And the puzzle revolved around the north wing.

Clearly that blackened, ruined part of the house was the source of Orielle's fears. But why? It was understandable that she should hate it after the terrible tragedy, but Aline felt certain there was far more to her terrors than that. Then there were Orlando's cryptic words: *No one's going to hurt Aline or me. Not now.* It suggested that Orlando, too, might be in danger, and that there was some connection with the past. What secret did the north wing hold? What horror haunted Orielle's memory and filled her with fear? And what was the connection with Aline's own eerie experiences since she had arrived in this house?

Aline knew that she could have no peace of mind until the mystery was solved, and she came to a decision. She would say nothing to anyone, not even to Orlando. But she would find out the truth. And her quest would begin with a search of the north wing.

Several days passed before Aline could carry out her plan. However, there was so much to occupy her that she had little time to fret.

Orlando's birthday ball was now only a week away, and the house was bustling with activity. Aline's new gown was nearly finished, and her dancing lessons with Orielle were progressing well. Orielle seemed to have shaken off her terrors in the wake of her conversation with Orlando. She had thrown herself exuberantly into the preparations and appeared cheerful and light-hearted. If, from time to time, a shadow crept across her face, it lasted only a few moments before she cast it aside and was happy once more.

There had been no more strange incidents – but Aline was still having uneasy moments. Now and then she felt a sudden urge to look over her shoulder, as though someone was watching her from the shadows. There was never anyone there, and she told herself that it was simply Orielle's bouts of disquiet making her nervous, too. But the feelings persisted. And sometimes, when she passed by a mirror, she thought she caught a glimpse of a reflection that was somehow out of place . . .

Then, three days before the party, Orlando announced that he had to go away.

'It's a great nuisance,' he said to Aline and Orielle at dinner, 'but it's a matter of business and so can't be helped. I'll be back in time for the ball, but you'll have to complete the preparations without me.'

Aline knew that, since his father's death, Orlando had run the family estate himself, and he took his responsibilities very seriously. She smiled at him across the table. 'Don't worry,' she told him. 'Orielle and I will manage very well.'

'And we'll look after each other,' Orielle added firmly.

Orlando gave them both a loving look, his gaze resting longer on Aline's face. 'I know you will,' he said.

They waved him off early the next morning. After he had gone Orielle seemed a little dejected. She hadn't slept well, she said, and asked Aline if she would mind not having a dancing lesson today.

'Of course not,' Aline replied, then: 'Orielle, are you all right?'

Orielle frowned. 'Yes. I just . . .' Suddenly she looked up at Aline. 'I just hope Orlando will be safe!'

'Why ever shouldn't he be?'

'Oh . . . no reason. I'm being silly; take no notice of me.'

'He isn't travelling far,' Aline reassured her. 'And he'll be back very soon.'

'Yes. Yes, he will. Besides, he's going away from the house, so . . .' Orielle's voice trailed off and she suppressed a little shiver. 'There's nothing to worry about. Nothing at all.'

There was a pause. Aline couldn't fathom Orielle's strange words and didn't know what to say. But then Orielle spoke again.

'I feel very tired. I think I'd like to rest until lunchtime. Would you ask the servants to take me to my room, please, Aline?'

Aline watched as Orielle was carried upstairs. Her peculiar remark had brought back the memory of the conversation she had overheard, and a chilly little feeling was taking root inside her. Orlando, and danger . . . *but he's going away from the house*, Orielle had said. As if the peril lurked here and nowhere else.

She realized then that she had the chance she had been waiting for. Orlando had gone away, Orielle was in her bedroom. For the first time she could explore the north wing without anyone knowing. And perhaps she might at last find the answers she was looking for.

Mrs Rosell was in the ballroom on the other side of the house; Aline could hear her voice giving instructions for the placing of newly arrived flower garlands. None of the other servants would question her, so, quickly and quietly, Aline made for the back stairs.

CHAPTER VI

ALINE HAD NEVER before ventured into the passage that led to the north wing. But as soon as she entered it, she felt a disturbing sense of familiarity . . . for everything was just as it had been in her last nightmare. The colours were the same. The emptiness. The shut door with its charred edges.

She felt queasy as she approached the door, and almost hoped that it would be locked, so she couldn't go through. But that was cowardly, she told herself sternly. Ignoring her quickening pulse, she reached out and tried the handle.

It turned. The door creaked open, and Aline gazed on a scene of utter desolation.

The fire had destroyed everything it touched, and the wing was a grim wilderness of blackened walls, charred and broken beams and shattered, gaping windows through which the morning light slanted coldly and dismally. And the floor . . . it was thick with rubble and debris, the flotsam of once-treasured furnishings burned beyond recognition to a waste of ash. Dust rose in sluggish eddies as Aline took a step forward, and despite the glassless windows there was a stale and musty smell in the air.

More daylight showed above and, looking up, Aline saw that there were great holes in the roof. Some of the timbers had collapsed as they burned, bringing tiles down with them. In places they had smashed through the floor, so that she could see through the wreckage of the boards to ground level. She would have to be very careful; one unwary step could easily send her plummeting down. Cautiously, she ventured in.

The scorched boards creaked alarmingly under her feet, but the floor seemed safe enough provided she avoided the gaps. Aline picked her way carefully among the debris, coughing sometimes as the clouds of dust got into her throat. She was horrified yet fascinated by the scene around her. It was so poignantly sad, especially when she began to find remnants from the past, little things that somehow had survived the fire. A silver thimble. A lady's satin shoe, charred but still intact. And the remains of a small painting, almost burned to nothing but with one piece still remaining, enough to show her that it had been a portrait of Orlando and Orielle as children.

But for all these tiny, pitiful relics, there was nothing that helped her to solve her own mystery. Until, picking her way gingerly through what had once been a door to another room, Aline saw something hanging on a wall ahead of her.

She stopped and stared. The object was rectangular in shape, and very large; taller than she was, in fact. And it was covered by a cloth. Another painting? Aline started towards it . . . then abruptly halted again. A cloth? An *undamaged* cloth? That could only mean that it had been covered up *after* the fire. But why?

Pushing down a sudden surge of excitement, and telling herself that it might be nothing at all, Aline hurried towards her new discovery. Yes, the cloth *was* new. Reaching up, she caught hold of it. It fell away, bringing a shower of cobwebs and ash with it –

Aline found herself confronting a huge, empty frame.

She frowned, baffled. Unlike the rest of the north wing's contents the frame was relatively undamaged. Traces of gilding showed clearly through the scorched blackness. *Had* it contained a portrait? Or –

Then she saw that there were shards of broken glass at the frame's edge, embedded in the rim. It was a mirror.

Something glittered suddenly at Aline's feet, making her start. She looked down, and saw that there was more glass littering the floor at the frame's foot, large pieces, half hidden among the dust and ashes. She looked at the frame again. She had seen one very like it before, she was certain.

And then she remembered her dream.

Aline took a rapid step back, almost tripped on something, regained her balance, and stared in dawning horror at the smashed mirror. In the nightmare she had opened the door to the north wing and someone had attacked her, pouncing at her from inside a mirror that came toppling out of the darkness. *This was that same mirror*.

A wave of icy coldness washed over her, and with a huge effort she forced herself to be calm. She had stumbled on something – but this discovery posed far more questions than it answered. The mirror was broken, its pieces scattered on the floor. How had that happened – during the fire, or in some other way? Why had it been covered up? Who had taken the trouble to shroud it, as though it were something precious that had to be preserved? And one more question; though Aline believed she already knew the answer. Was this where the glass under her pillow had come from?

She looked down at the shards lying near her feet; then swiftly bent and picked two of them up. She didn't want to stay in the north wing a moment longer. The grim atmosphere was starting to make her very uneasy, and she had an irrational but compelling feeling that she wasn't *entirely* alone. She didn't believe in ghosts – or so she tried to convince herself – but she couldn't shake off the sense that she was being watched.

Carrying the pieces of the broken mirror carefully, Aline made her way as fast as she could back to the door and the haven of the house beyond. By the time she reached it she was breathless, and she didn't dare look back as she shut the door behind her. Along the passage, quickly, and by a back way to her own room. There, she took the piece of glass that had cut her from its hiding place, and laid it on the bed beside the two from the north wing. The silvered backings were identical. All three pieces were from the same mirror.

Aline was so engrossed by her discovery that she didn't hear her name being called from outside. When the door opened she jumped like a startled cat – and turned to see Orielle looking at her from the threshold.

'Aline?' Orielle wheeled herself into the room. 'Whatever's the matter? You're as white as –' She stopped. She had seen the glass shards.

Aline started to say, 'Orielle, I don't –' but Orielle cut across her, her voice rising in horror.

'Where did you get those?' She pushed herself forward, frantically, and made a grab for Aline's arm. 'Where did you get them? *Aline, where have you been?*'

On the verge of a quickly invented lie, Aline realized that she couldn't deny the truth. There was ash on her hands, cobwebs on her dress – they betrayed the truth as surely as the glass, and she had no choice but to confess what she had done.

To her dismay, as soon as Orielle heard the story she burst into tears.

'Orielle!' Distressed, Aline went to comfort her, but Orielle pushed her violently away.

'Why did you have to be such a fool?' she cried furiously. 'No one is allowed to go near the north wing – you were told that when you came here, you *knew* it! You had no right to meddle!'

She was so unreasonable that Aline too became angry. 'After what happened to me, I think I had every right!' she retorted.

Orielle's sobbing stopped, and her eyes widened. 'What do you mean?' Suddenly her face was haggard. 'What's happened? *Tell me!*'

Aware that she couldn't back down now, Aline told her everything. About the nightmares. The hate-filled, whispering voice. The threats. And, finally, about the glass under her pillow. Orielle listened in silence. When Aline stopped speaking her face was stark and still . . . and Aline saw something else in her expression. Something that gave her away.

She said sharply, 'Orielle . . . you know, don't you? You know who it is that's trying to frighten me!'

Orielle stared at her. There was a long pause. Then she said in a very small voice, 'Yes, I do know.' Another silence. 'It's Zilla.'

'Zilla?' Aline had never heard the name before. 'Who is Zilla?'

Orielle gazed back at her. Her face was sombre, her eyes huge and troubled . . . and bitter.

'Zilla was a servant here,' she said. 'Three years ago she came looking for work.' She shuddered as though at an ugly memory. 'She had no home, and my mother took pity on her. I only wish she hadn't been so kind. I only wish . . .' She choked, put a hand to her mouth, then added with sudden vehemence, '*I only wish that that monstrous, evil creature had never been allowed to set foot in this house!*'

CHAPTER VII

'IT WASN'T LONG before we knew that Zilla was going to bring trouble,' Orielle said. 'She was very beautiful; she had flame-coloured hair, a great mane of it, and a lovely face, though something about it was cruel and haughty. And she knew how good-looking she was; she used to spend hours just admiring her own reflection.' Orielle gave a funny, broken little laugh. 'You might say she was obsessed with mirrors, for she could never pass one without stopping to gaze at herself. She should have been rebuked, of course, for she wasted so much time when she should have been doing her work. But everyone was too afraid of her to say anything.'

'Afraid?' Aline echoed. 'She was only a servant . . .'

'She was more than that,' Orielle said darkly. 'She hadn't been here long when a rumour started that she had magical powers. That she was a witch.' She shivered. 'We thought it was nonsense at first. We should have listened.'

'What happened?' Aline asked.

'Zilla loved the fact that people were afraid of her. She played on it to get things she wanted, or

to avoid the tasks she didn't want to do. And . . .
then she saw Orlando.'

Orlando had been away travelling – but as
soon as he returned, the real trouble started.
From the moment Zilla set eyes on him, she
wanted him. And, at first, Orlando was very attracted to her. No one could blame him, Orielle
said with bitter anger in her voice, for Zilla's
beauty was enough to captivate any man. Orielle
and her parents tried to warn him about her real
nature, but Orlando was too enchanted to take
any notice.

Then after a while Orlando began to realize
that Zilla was not quite what she seemed. Con-
vinced that he was completely under her sway,
she became arrogant and impudent, putting on
airs and behaving as if she was mistress of the
house – which she thought she would be one day,
for she was determined to marry Orlando. But
Orlando's eyes were opening to the truth, and at
last, despite Zilla's increasingly frenzied efforts
to hold on to him, his infatuation turned to re-
pulsion and he told her that he wanted nothing
more to do with her.

And that was when the spate of 'accidents'
began.

'They were only little things at first,' said Orielle. 'Father slipped on the stairs for no reason,
and twisted his ankle. Mother was driving in the
carriage when a wheel came loose and she almost
crashed. A wasp attacked me – it wasn't the

season for wasps – and stung my face. All of us kept having mishaps – all, that is, except for Orlando. He seemed immune somehow, and that was too much of a coincidence. We started to believe the tales about Zilla. We suspected that she *was* a witch, and that she was using her powers against anyone who stood between her and what she wanted. The trouble was, we couldn't prove anything. Until late one night Mother went down to the kitchen and found Zilla in the pantry. She was mixing a potion; she didn't realize anyone else was there, and Mother heard her chanting as she worked. It was a spell – a spell designed to kill someone. And on the table beside her was a bottle of Father's favourite wine.'

Aline let out a long, slow breath. 'What did your mother do?'

'She confronted Zilla,' said Orielle. 'There was a *terrible* quarrel. Father came running, and I could hear them all shouting from the hall; then Father threw Zilla out of the house and promised to set his dogs on her if she ever came near us again.' She gave another, greater shudder. 'I can hear it all in my mind now. The dogs snarling on their leashes, Father shouting, Zilla screaming furious threats –'

'Threats?'

'Oh, yes. She didn't accept her defeat, you see. She swore that she'd have revenge on us for thwarting her. We'd all be sorry, she said. And . . . and if she couldn't have Orlando, then no other girl ever would. She promised that. She *promised* it.'

Aline stared at Orielle in dread as a glimmer of the truth began to form in her mind. Orielle had taken a deep breath as if to calm herself; now she swallowed and continued with her story.

The family had told themselves that Zilla's threats were just empty words. But they were wrong – for a few weeks later, when the household was asleep, she came back.

'I woke up in the middle of the night,' Orielle said, 'and I smelled smoke. I ran to the door, and when I opened it and looked out I saw that the far end of the passage was on fire.' She swallowed again. 'I just *screamed*. It woke Orlando, and as he came out of his room we both heard a hideous sound. Laughter – wild and triumphant laughter – and then we saw Zilla. She was running along the corridor; she had a burning torch in her hand, and as she ran she was setting fire to anything and everything she could reach.'

Orlando and Orielle gave chase. But they couldn't catch Zilla, for she had the strength and speed of madness, and even when the servants came racing to help, she eluded them all. The entire wing was on fire now, and suddenly they realized that their parents were in terrible danger, for flames were raging through the passage to their bedroom, and they were still on the far side!

'We started to run back to find them,' Orielle said. 'But by then the roof was blazing too, and suddenly a beam collapsed. The last thing I re-membered was seeing it crashing towards me . . . I heard myself scream, and then everything went black. When I came to, I was lying in the garden with the servants around me. They said the fall-ing beam had trapped me, and that Orlando had pulled me clear just in time and carried me to safety. But our parents . . .' Her voice caught. 'He couldn't reach them. No one could. The fire had too great a hold.'

It was only later, when she started to recover, that Orielle had heard the rest of the grim story. Orlando, in a frenzy of grief, had tried to plunge back into the burning wing. He wanted to find Zilla and kill her, but the servants dragged him back. No one would stand a chance in that in-ferno, they said. They would find Zilla – or what was left of her – when it was over.

The north wing burned all night, but finally the fire was extinguished. Next day, his face dead-white and his eyes granite-hard with rage, Orlando searched for Zilla, and found her. She was lying among the ashes, at the foot of a great mirror that hung on the wall, and by a miracle, was almost completely undamaged. Zilla too, in-credibly, was hardly touched by the flames. Her face was fixed in a demented, triumphant and delighted expression, and Orlando had the hor-rible impression that she had been gazing into the mirror, gazing at herself, in the moments before the fire overcame her.

As Orielle said this, Aline felt a sickening inward jolt, and she interrupted. 'Orielle, wait. *Wait*. Are you saying that Zilla was . . . *dead*?'

Orielle stared sombrely back at her. 'Oh, yes. She was dead.'

'But . . . if she died, how can she . . .'

'Be behind the attacks on you?' Orielle smiled a strange, terrible smile. 'You don't know all the story yet, Aline.'

Orlando, Orielle said, had bent to touch Zilla, wanting to be certain that she really was dead. As he did so, a soft laugh echoed in the burned-out room. Shocked, he looked up . . . and saw Zilla's reflection standing in the mirror. She was gazing out at him with a contemptuous smile on her face. As Orlando stared in disbelief, she laughed again, a dreadful laugh, and he heard her voice.

'Did you think you were rid of me?' she said. 'You're wrong, Orlando. I once swore that if I can't have you, no other girl ever will – and I meant it. Be very careful. For if you ever fall in love, I'll be back. *I'll be back!*'

In a storm of grief and loathing, Orlando smashed the mirror. Zilla's image shattered away, and her last peal of laughter faded and died into silence. But her curse rang in his mind; and, Orielle said miserably, with good reason. For now it had come true. Zilla had returned – and they were all in danger.

For a long time the two girls were silent.

Aline was struggling to take in what she had heard. The story seemed incredible, impossible; yet deep down she knew it was true. For she had seen the flame-haired girl in her dream, and had heard her mocking voice and the threats she made. There could be no doubt. Zilla was back. And she meant to do everything in her power to wreck the love between Aline and Orlando.

At last, Orielle spoke again. In a small, shrivelled voice she said, 'Aline, there's only one thing to do. For Orlando's sake you've got to go away and forget him.'

'*What?*' Aline was stunned. 'I won't do that. I can't!'

'You must. Don't you see? If you stay, it'll only get worse. Zilla is too powerful to fight, and I won't have Orlando's life put in danger!'

'But there has to be a way to defeat her,' Aline argued. 'I won't abandon Orlando – I love him too much, and I'll fight for him!'

They quarrelled bitterly then. Orielle was terrified of Zilla and of what she might do. If Aline stayed, she said, Orlando would be in deadly peril, and she would not allow that under any circumstances. Nothing Aline could say would sway her; Aline *must* go, for if she didn't, another terrible tragedy would befall them before long. And at last, when Aline continued to argue, Orielle lost her temper and said furiously that if she refused to leave of her own free will, she would *make* her go. She was still Aline's employer, and Aline had to obey her.

At last, angrily, they parted. When Orielle wheeled herself away to her room with tears streaming down her face Aline wanted to go after her and make peace, but thought it better to wait a while, to give them both a chance to calm down.

However, when she tried Orielle's door later it was locked, and Mrs Rosell said Orielle had given instructions that she wasn't to be disturbed. With a sigh Aline returned to her own room. Perhaps Orielle would feel differently tomorrow. If she didn't, then Aline didn't know what to do. For in truth Orielle *was* her employer, and must be obeyed. If she ordered her to go, then go she must. But she couldn't bear to lose Orlando. She simply couldn't bear it!

Aline went to bed that night feeling desperately unhappy. Her joy was in ashes, and her beautiful ball gown, nearly finished now and draped over a chair, seemed to mock her anguish. But then, shortly after midnight, she woke again . . . and heard someone softly calling her name.

With a start, she sat up in bed. The night was dark, but on the far side of the room a faint oval of light was glowing. It seemed to be shining from her mirror – and as Aline watched, a face began to take form in the glass. A girl, with fiery red hair, and eyes that glittered venomously. The mouth beneath those scornful eyes smiled a cruel smile. And Zilla's voice hissed malevolently, eerily through the room.

'*Just wait, Aline. Just wait!*'

Anger swamped Aline's fear, and the sheer strength of it galvanized her. She sprang out of bed and was across the room in three strides, confronting the ghostly image in the glass.

'I'm not afraid of you!' she cried defiantly. 'And if you think you're going to take Orlando away from me, you're wrong. Whatever it takes, whatever I have to do, I'll defeat you!'

The face in the mirror twisted and distorted, and Zilla flung back her head and laughed. The sound of it pealed wildly through Aline's skull – then the light flared violently, the image vanished, and Aline was left staring at her own wide-eyed reflection.

Slowly, half expecting Zilla to reappear, Aline backed away. Nothing happened. The witch-girl was gone. But the memory of her threat echoed in Aline's mind. Zilla was out for revenge. She would be back . . .

Aline fell into a troubled sleep. She thought she would have more bad dreams, but to her surprise nothing troubled her until she woke the next morning. The sun was streaming in at her window; she started to get up . . . then stopped.

Where was her ball gown? It had been on the chair last night but now it had vanished. Frowning, Aline looked around the room. And then she saw it.

Her beautiful dress had been screwed up and thrown on the floor. With a cry Aline ran to pick it up, and as she shook out the crumpled folds her eyes widened as she saw what had been done to it.

The skirt was slashed from top to bottom, as though someone had attacked it in a mad fit of rage. Aline stared at the tattered remnants, too horrified even to think clearly –

And with a little clink, something fell out of the skirt on to the floor.

It was another piece of glass from the mirror in the north wing. Zilla had issued her challenge.

CHAPTER VIII

ALINE'S HEART WAS pounding as she strode along the passage that led to the north wing. She was keyed-up and nervous, but she was also filled with an unshakeable resolve. Zilla thought she could intimidate her as she had intimidated Orielle. But she was wrong. Aline was about to prove that to her beyond any doubt. She had taken a hammer from the woodshed when the gardener wasn't looking, and she was going to smash the glass shards from the shrouded mirror, shatter and grind them until they were nothing more than dust. That mirror was Zilla's doorway into the living world. Aline meant to ensure that she could never use it again.

The door was ahead of her. She marched up to it, grasped the handle – but the door wouldn't open. It had been locked.

'No!' Furiously Aline tugged at the handle, twisting and turning it and rattling the door with all her strength. It was useless; the lock was too strong. Then, as she wrestled with it, hurrying footsteps sounded in the corridor behind her.

'What's all this commotion?' It was Mrs Rosell, looking surprised and indignant. 'Aline! Whatever are you doing here?'

Aline tried desperately to think of an excuse, but the housekeeper was already starting to scold her. She knew perfectly well that no one was allowed to go into the north wing! It was dangerous; she might easily fall through the floor and break her neck! Besides, Mrs Rosell added sternly, Miss Orielle had given orders this very morning that the door was to be kept locked from now on. So Aline would oblige her by coming away at once.

Aline went reluctantly back to the main house. *Orielle's* orders . . . she must have suspected that Aline would try to defy her. Well, Aline thought, she wouldn't let matters rest there. She would confront Orielle and *make* her hand over the key!

Orielle was already downstairs, where breakfast had been laid in the dining-room. When Aline walked in Orielle tensed visibly. Aline told her what had happened, and demanded the key to the locked door.

Orielle went white about the lips. 'Certainly not!' she said. 'You've caused enough trouble already, and I won't let you cause any more!'

They started to argue again, and the quarrel was growing heated when suddenly the door opened. The girls stopped, turned, and saw Orlando standing on the threshold.

'Orlando!' Aline ran to him and flung her arms around his neck. 'Oh, Orlando, you're back!'

'I finished my business early,' Orlando said. 'And I couldn't wait to get home.' Then he held

Aline at arm's length and gazed worriedly into her eyes. 'But what's going on? You sounded as if you were quarrelling!'

They told him everything. Orielle begged him to make Aline leave, while Aline protested her determination not to give in to Zilla's threats. Orlando listened to them both, his handsome face growing grave.

'Aline,' he said gently, 'I'd like to talk to Orielle alone for a few minutes. Would you mind?'

Aline's pulse quickened. Did this mean that he was going to do what his sister wanted? She opened her mouth to protest. But something in Orlando's look stilled her tongue, so, uneasily, she nodded and left the room.

She was never to know what Orlando said to Orielle during the few minutes they were alone. But when he emerged from the dining-room, his face was resolute.

'My love,' he said, 'I understand Orielle's fear. But you're right and she's wrong, and I've told her so. If we don't stand up to Zilla now, her shadow will follow us all for the rest of our lives. I won't have that. And I won't lose you, Aline. Whatever the danger, we'll meet it and defy her.'

Relief flooded through Aline, and with it an ache of love. 'Oh, Orlando . . .' She caught hold of his hands. 'But what about Orielle? She's so very afraid.'

'I know. But we'll help her. And at the ball . . .' Orlando smiled, though it took an effort. 'We'll all join together, and show Zilla that we're too strong to be defeated!'

With the ball due to take place on the following night, they all had too much to occupy them to allow any time for brooding. Orielle was subdued and tearful after her talk with Orlando, but she was striving to keep her terrors at bay. As she confessed to Aline later, it wasn't that she didn't approve of the betrothal; very far from it, for she already loved Aline like a sister. But she was so afraid of Zilla, and of what she might do. Aline understood, and tried to reassure her. But in her own heart she wasn't as confident as she pretended. Despite all the brave words that had been spoken, there was an uneasy atmosphere in the house as the last preparations got under way. Zilla's threats seemed to hang over them like a malignant cloud, and the fact that there were no more strange incidents only added to the tension. Zilla would do something, they were certain. But what? It was like waiting for a storm to break – but with no idea of when or where the first lightning bolt would strike.

They all went to bed that night in trepidation. No one slept well, but still there was no sign of trouble, and Orlando's birthday dawned with a bright sunrise that seemed determined to banish the shadows. As the morning wore on the house became busier and busier. Every room seemed to be a hive of activity as decorations were completed, food laid out and everything made ready for the arrival of the first guests.

Aline's gown had been hastily repaired, and the damage to the skirt had been disguised so that it might never have existed. Nonethcless, Aline could not help a chilly shiver of unease as, late in the afternoon, she began to get ready for the ball. Still Zilla had made no move. But Aline could feel her brooding influence, and knew that the lull would not last.

Mrs Rosell helped her into the gown, exclaiming as she fastened it that Aline would turn every head in the ballroom. Aline stared at herself in the mirror. She looked transformed. She *felt* transformed. And suddenly an overwhelming sense of happiness burst through the threatening clouds in her mind, so that she gave Mrs Rosell a radiant smile. Tonight, she would pledge herself to Orlando. And if happiness could bring beauty, then she would be the most beautiful girl in the entire world!

She slipped on the gold satin shoes that Orielle had lent her, then fastened the necklace and bracelet of emeralds – also Orielle's – around her throat and wrist. Mrs Rosell dressed her hair, brushing it until it shone and then piling it into glistening curls and fixing it with a jewelled comb. Gloves and a velvet wrap completed the picture, and as Aline cast the wrap on to her shoulders there was a knock on her door and Orielle was wheeled in by a maid.

Orielle looked breathtakingly lovely in a russet-gold dress trimmed with crimson, which lent a delicate colour to her pale cheeks. Looking at her, Aline felt sad that she would only be able to watch the dancing rather than joining in, but she masked her feelings, knowing that Orielle would hate to be pitied, and simply said, 'You look wonderful, Orielle! Orlando will be so proud.'

'He'll be prouder still of you,' Orielle said warmly, her eyes sparkling. 'And so am I.'

Strains of melody were drifting from the ballroom as the musicians hired for the evening began to tune up, and as the girls went out on to the landing together they heard a buzz of voices in the hall below. The guests were arriving. Orielle turned to Aline and smiled again.

'Don't be nervous,' she said. 'This is *your* night.' She paused. 'Are you ready?'

Aline returned a grateful look. 'Yes,' she said. 'I'm ready.'

Within an hour, Aline had forgotten Zilla, forgotten her nervousness; forgotten everything but the joy and excitement of the ball.

Orlando, magnificent in grey velvet, had met the two girls as they came down the stairs, and the light in his eyes when he looked at Aline made words unnecessary. Together they wheeled Orielle's chair into the ballroom, and to Aline it was like entering a new and fabulous world.

Lights blazed everywhere, reflecting in the great mirrors that lined the walls and turning the entire ballroom into a glittering fantasy. Between the mirrors hung garlands of leaves and flowers, and banks of more flowers adorned the white-clothed tables where food and wine and huge bowls of punch stood among piles of shining plates and glasses. As Orlando entered, a cheer went up from the throng of guests, and Aline had the dizzying impression of a moving sea of smiling faces, gorgeous colours and sparkling jewels as the company pressed forward to wish him a happy birthday. She was introduced to so many people; neighbours and friends from miles around, old and young alike – they must have invited everyone in the entire district, she thought giddily, and it was overwhelming! But with Orlando at her side she couldn't feel afraid, and soon she was laughing and talking with the rest.

The dancing began, and there was applause as Orlando led Aline on to the floor. Before long they were swept up in a whirl of lively music and swirling skirts and coats. Sometimes Aline glanced to where Orielle was sitting in her chair and felt a pang of sorrow. But Orielle looked happy, and was never short of attentive young men to talk to her and bring her food or drink, so Aline let herself concentrate on enjoying the dance.

They stopped for a rest after the third set and

went to join Orielle. Orielle was looking at another part of the room as they approached, and suddenly Aline saw her tense and lean forward in her chair.

'Orielle?' she said. Orielle started and looked round, and Aline added, 'What is it? What's wrong?'

Orielle glanced across the room again, eyes narrowed – then abruptly she relaxed and shook her head as though to clear it.

'Nothing,' she said. 'Just for a moment I thought . . . but I imagined it. It was a trick of the light.' And before Aline could ask what was a trick of the light, she changed the subject. But when Orlando went to fetch them both a glass of punch, Orielle watched him uneasily as he crossed the room. He stopped at the tables, and moments later Orielle said, 'Who's that he's talking to?'

Aline peered. 'The girl in the dark blue dress? He introduced me to her a while ago, but I can't remember her name.'

'Ah,' said Orielle with relief in her voice. 'It's a blue dress . . . yes, of course, I can see it better now.'

Aline frowned. 'Orielle, what's the matter?' she asked.

Orielle touched her tongue to her lips. 'You haven't . . . seen anyone in a *black* gown, have you?'

'Black?' Aline echoed. 'No. No girl would wear black to a ball, surely?'

'No. No, of course not. Forget it. Here's Orlando.' And again Orielle changed the subject as her brother joined them.

Aline and Orlando sat for half an hour with Orielle, then Orlando asked Aline to dance again. As they formed up with other couples, Aline saw something out of the corner of her eye. The flicker of a black skirt . . .

Her heart skipped and she stared into the crowd. The skirt had vanished now. But it *was* black; she was sure of it. And she remembered Orielle's fearful reaction . . .

The musicians struck up and the dance began, and for a few minutes Aline was too busy concentrating on her steps to think of anything else. Then, as the dance carried them into the centre of the ballroom, she suddenly saw the black gown again. It was on the far side of the room, and for one moment as the whirling couples moved aside she had a single, clear view.

It *was* a black gown. The girl wearing it was young and very beautiful, though there was something ruthless and almost repellent about her looks. Her hair wasn't piled up but swung loose about her shoulders. Red hair. Red as a flame. And on her face was a smile that made Aline's stomach churn. For she had seen that smile before.

Aline's skin began to crawl. She spun round and looked across the ballroom to where Orielle sat. Orielle was leaning forward in her chair, staring at the girl in black as though mesmerized, and on her face was a look of sheer horror.

Zilla had come to the ball.

CHAPTER IX

ORLANDO COULD ONLY stare in astonishment as, with no warning, Aline broke from him and forged her way through the crowd of dancers.

'Aline?' He called after her but she took no notice; she was running towards Orielle, and Orielle was beckoning urgently. Baffled and alarmed, Orlando started in her wake.

White-faced, Orielle grabbed hold of Aline's hand as she reached her. 'Did you *see*?'

'Yes!' Aline was breathless. 'It *was* Zilla, wasn't it?'

'It must have been; I don't know anyone else with hair like that. But –' Orielle looked wildly around. 'Now she's gone. I can't see her anywhere!'

They heard their names being called, and saw Orlando heading towards them. 'Aline, don't tell him!' Orielle whispered urgently. 'Not yet. Not until we're absolutely certain.'

Aline wasn't sure that was wise, but she nodded, and when Orlando arrived Orielle quickly made up an excuse. She had been waving to someone else, she said, and Aline had thought something was wrong. No, no; of course nothing was *really* wrong; Aline had just mistaken the gesture. Silly of her, Orielle said laughingly. They should go back and enjoy the rest of the dance.

Aline no longer felt like dancing. The incident had shaken her; she wanted a few minutes to recover before she ventured on to the floor again. And she also wanted to look for the girl in the black dress. So she asked Orlando if she might have some more punch, and Orielle, understanding, asked him to fetch some for her, too. As he went, Orielle caught hold of Aline's hand again.

'We must look carefully,' she said in a fervent whisper. 'Comb the room — you start at the left, I'll start at the right.'

Silence fell between them as they both peered into the crowd. The contrast between their unease and the lively, vivid world of the ball going on around them made Aline feel quite queasy, and she was wishing she hadn't eaten any food earlier when suddenly she saw the girl again.

She reached out to grab Orielle's arm and call, '*There!*' But in the instant before she did so, she realized with a shock that something was awry. She hadn't seen the real Zilla but only her reflection as she danced past one of the great, shining mirrors that lined the ballroom. Yet when she looked to where the girl herself should have been, there was no sign of her.

Heart pounding, Aline scanned the mirrors again. There — she was there, reflected in the glass between a thin, aristocratic-looking woman and a portly man in a red waistcoat. And there were the real man and woman in the room; she could see them clearly.

But Zilla was not between them . . .

With dawning horror Aline realized what was happening. Zilla wasn't actually in this room mingling with the guests. But she *had* come to the ball. She was inside the mirrors. And from the world within the glass she was smiling out at Aline, a smile of loathsome triumph.

In a tiny, cracked voice Orielle said, '*Aline* . . .' and Aline knew that she, too, had seen and realized. Zilla's image had vanished again, and suddenly Orielle put both hands up to her face in alarm.

'Where's Orlando?' she cried. 'There can't be any doubt now – we have to warn him!'

Aline looked swiftly for Orlando and saw him talking to two elderly men by one of the tables. She let out a sigh of relief and said, 'We mustn't let anyone else think anything's wrong. We'll tell him quietly, as soon as he comes back.'

Orielle nodded, and for another minute they scanned the room for any further sign of Zilla. But she didn't reappear. And Orlando had not yet returned.

'I wish he'd hurry,' Orielle said nervously. 'I can't bear . . .' Then her voice trailed off and her eyes widened. 'Aline, I can't see him! I can't see Orlando! *Where's he gone?*'

Aline looked. There was no one at the table now. Orlando had vanished.

And then Orielle uttered a choked, terrible sound and pointed across the ballroom.

Orlando was among the dancing couples on the far side of the room. With him, gripping his hand and his waist in a hideous parody of the dance, was Zilla.

Orielle's face bleached. 'She's come out of the mirror! She's come after him!' Frantically she started to push her chair forward, but Aline was faster. She plunged into the throng, barging people but not pausing to apologize, fighting her way towards Orlando as a wave of terror and fury rose in her mind. Orlando's face was a mask of shock; he looked stunned and unable to resist Zilla's influence. Then he saw Aline, and the spell snapped. Furiously he twisted in Zilla's grasp, trying to break her hold on him. But Zilla still had hold of his fingers; suddenly and violently she pulled him off balance, and the two of them spun together towards the very edge of the room. Towards one of the mirrors –

The dance was so lively and boisterous now that none of the other couples had noticed anything amiss. But Aline saw what was about to happen, and there was nothing she could do to prevent it. Zilla reached the mirror, with Orlando still struggling. For a moment they teetered. Then in one quick movement Zilla stepped *through* the glass, and dragged Orlando with her.

The mirror's surface swirled like windswept water. For a moment everything in it was obscured. Then it cleared, and Orlando and Zilla appeared again. They were gone from the ballroom. They were inside the glass.

As though in a waking nightmare, Aline stared transfixed at the terrible, impossible sight of Orlando trapped within the mirror. He could see out, she knew, for he had freed himself from Zilla's clutches and was clawing at the glass, striving to smash down its barrier. But his efforts were in vain. Zilla's power had pulled him into the mirror, but he couldn't break through it again and return to the real world. Behind him Zilla was laughing, though the sound of it couldn't be heard. And as Orlando's gaze locked with Aline's, she saw his lips move in a silent, desperate plea for help.

Suddenly Zilla snatched Orlando's arm. She pulled him away, and they vanished into the mirror world. Only Aline and Orielle saw them go, and the music and dancing flowed on as though nothing had happened. Aline had seen which way Zilla had dragged Orlando, and a wild idea came to her.

She swung round and forged her way back to Orielle. Orielle was frantic, but there was no time for explanations; Aline simply grabbed hold of the wheelchair, swung it round and pushed the protesting Orielle towards the doors.

'Aline!' Orielle cried. 'Aline, what are you doing?'

'Hush!' Aline pushed away the hands that batted at her. The doors stood open; breaking into a run she propelled the chair out into the entrance hall.

Lamps burned in their sconces on the walls, lighting the empty hall. And in a tall mirror by the staircase, Orlando and Zilla were visible.

Orielle gave a cry of despair. Orlando and Zilla were struggling, and even as they watched, Zilla – whose strength in the mirror world seemed unhuman – pulled her captive away and out of sight again. But now Orielle realized what Aline had already understood. The world in which Orlando was trapped was a mirror version of the house. If Aline and Orielle could keep track of him through the real house, then there might be a chance to save him from Zilla!

'Quickly!' In frustration and panic Orielle beat at the arms of her chair. 'Follow them – oh hurry, Aline, *hurry*!'

So began a waking nightmare that, for Aline, was like reliving the terrible dream she had had. Through rooms and passages she and Orielle followed the fleeting reflections of Orlando and Zilla. With servants and guests all in the ball-room there was no one to see them and no one to help them, and as the wheelchair rattled peril-ously along it seemed that all their efforts would be fruitless, for Zilla was always one step ahead of them. Sometimes Aline thought she heard the echoes of distant, mad laughter ringing through the house as the flame-haired girl mocked their endeavours, and once she seemed to hear Orlando's voice, faint and faraway, calling her name. But though every mirror they passed showed a tantalizing glimpse of their quarry, they could never catch up.

At last the chase brought them back to the hall, and they stumbled to a halt. Aline was gasping with fatigue from pushing the chair, while Orielle sobbed with fear and the frustration of her own helplessness. They both felt they could go no further ... but then something moved in the mirror at the foot of the stairs.

'Orlando!' Aline gasped. He had freed himself from Zilla and was there in the glass, gazing out at them and gesturing wildly. His lips moved and Aline knew he was trying to tell them something, but she couldn't hear his voice and she shook her head frantically.

Orlando understood. He stopped trying to call, and instead pointed urgently towards the stairs. Then his hands formed the shape of a door, and he traced the letter 'N' in the air.

'"N"...' Orielle said bewilderedly – then suddenly light dawned. '"N" for North! The north wing! That's what he's trying to tell us!'

'The shrouded mirror ...' Aline gasped. Of

course; of *course*! Zilla's doorway between worlds –

Then, in the mirror, Zilla came into view. Orlando saw her; he flung one last, desperate, pleading glance out of the glass, then turned and ran. The girls saw him reach the reflection of the staircase, saw Zilla rushing in pursuit, and as they both disappeared Aline whirled to face Orielle.

'The mirror in the north wing is the key to Zilla's power!' she cried. 'She used it – or her spirit did – to escape from the fire two years ago, and it's the strongest of all her doorways between worlds. We have to use it, Orielle. We have to use it to get Orlando back!'

Orielle gasped, hope filling her face as she understood . . . then an instant later joy turned to despair. 'But the mirror's broken,' she protested. 'Orlando smashed it!'

'Then we must mend it!'

They stared at each other. Then footsteps sounded behind them. Orielle twisted round in her chair and saw two menservants coming from the direction of the ballroom.

'Jarus! Reeth!' she called to them, and there was new resolve in her voice. 'Come quickly – carry me upstairs!'

CHAPTER X

THE CHASE BEGAN, but this time with a purpose as the wheelchair bumped along the carpeted landings of the house's upper floor. As they passed yet more mirrors Aline and Orielle caught fresh glimpses of Orlando and sometimes of Zilla, but their earlier fear was eclipsed now by fierce determination.

Then, as they neared the corridor that led to the north wing, Orielle suddenly gave a cry of horror, and pointed.

Ahead of them was another mirror, and in its depths a hot light was flaring.

'Oh, no!' Aline's eyes widened in shock, and the chair skidded to a halt as both girls stared, appalled. Beyond the glass, flames were leaping – the mirror-house was on fire! And in the mirror, dramatically framed by the glaring light, stood Zilla. She was holding a burning brand in her hand, gazing out at them with searing contempt and hatred. Clouds of smoke coiled thickly behind her, and Aline and Orielle heard her voice as though from a great distance.

'No one else shall ever have Orlando! No one!'

Orielle let out a wail of despair, and with the energy of sheer desperation Aline pushed the chair in a perilous, breakneck run towards the north wing. Just one more corridor – but there was fire in all the mirrors now, leaping and flickering, and Zilla's wild laughter seemed to din in their ears. They raced along the last passage; the charred door was ahead of them and Orielle fumbled for the key. She pushed it into the lock; the door swung open and Aline thrust the chair forward –

The chair stopped dead and would not move. Aline had forgotten the debris that littered the north wing's floor, but now she realized to her dismay that the wheelchair couldn't possibly get through. There was no time to spare; if she stopped to clear the way, the fire in the mirror world would take too great a hold and Orlando would be in deadly danger.

'Orielle, I can't get through!' she cried. 'I'll have to go on alone!'

'*No!*' Orielle screamed. Her hands gripped the chair arms. 'I've got to get there! I *will* get there!' Aline saw her arm muscles strain, and suddenly she was upright, still gripping the chair but standing on her feet. She swayed, and tremulously thrust one foot forward. 'Help me, Aline!'

Aline caught her as she seemed about to collapse, and Orielle stumbled out of the chair. She was no great weight; she could stand even if she couldn't walk, and wildly Aline thought, *We can do it – surely we can do it!*

Clinging to Aline, half stumbling and half

dragged, Orielle started across the littered floor. It was a perilous route, through darkness and with obstacles at every turn, but they struggled on together. And then they saw a gleam of bright, orange light ahead.

'It's the broken mirror!' Orielle cried.

Aline saw that she was right. The shards of the shrouded mirror that littered the floor were ablaze with firelight – and now the blaze had a powerful hold. They fought their way over the last few treacherous steps, then Aline let go and with a gasp Orielle collapsed on to the floor in front of the mirror's frame.

'The cloth!' she called out. 'Take off the cloth!'

She was scrabbling frantically to gather the broken pieces of glass together, and Aline darted to the mirror and snatched the covering away. She wrestled with the heavy frame until it leaned at an angle against the wall, then feverishly she and Orielle started to fit the broken shards together.

It was a horrifying race against time. Fumbling in their haste and desperation, the girls fought to rebuild the broken mirror. The pieces were big enough to enable them to work out where each should go, but still the mirror seemed to grow agonizingly slowly. And the glare of light was growing, too. The fire in the other world was spreading rapidly; beyond the glass all was now a mayhem of flame and smoke. They could see no sign of Orlando, but the distant sound of Zilla's crazed laughter echoed in the air around them.

The mirror was almost whole again. Only three small gaps remained to be filled, and Orielle's urgency flowered to panic as she searched through the rubble on the floor.

'I can't find any more!'

'What?' Aline swung round.

'There's nothing else here! We've used all the pieces and the mirror isn't complete! Oh, Aline –'

'Wait!' Suddenly Aline remembered. The shard under her pillow – it was still in her room! And she had taken two others to compare it with –

'I know where they are!' Oh, she was such a *fool* not to have thought of them earlier. There was so little time left . . .

'I'll be back!' Not pausing to explain any more, she ran towards the door. Down the passage, racing, racing, skidding round the corner and away to her bedroom. The shards were here, they *had* to be here! Panting with breathlessness and terror Aline flung things about in her frantic search. Then she saw something glinting.

'*Ah!*' She pounced like a hunting terrier, snatched up the pieces and was out of the door and away back to the north wing. As she burst in she could see the fire blazing in the mirror, spreading a gory light across the desolate scene. Orielle was silhouetted by the glow, and as she saw Aline she beckoned frenziedly. 'Hurry, Aline, hurry!'

Three last pieces. Would they fit, would they

complete the jigsaw? Aline's heart hammered as she pressed them into place –

And the mirror was whole.

In one stunning moment the light of the fire in the mirror world redoubled, blazing out into the real world in a huge flare. As if the completion of the mirror had broken down the barriers, the sound of crackling flames roared out of the glass, and the sharp tang of smoke filled their nostrils. But where was Orlando? Orielle had pulled herself to her knees and was shouting his name into the glass, but there was no answering cry from the burning house.

'It's useless!' Aline cried. 'He can't hear you!' There was only one thing to do, she knew it with a dreadful certainty. And though the thought terrified her, she had to do it. For Orlando's sake, for his life, she *had* to.

'Orielle, hold my hand.' She grasped Orielle's fingers. 'Whatever you do, don't let go!'

Orielle realized what she intended. 'Aline, you can't!'

'I must.' Before her nerve could fail her Aline pushed against the mirror. She expected it to give way, for the barrier to break. But it didn't; all she felt was cold, unyielding glass.

'*No!*' Fury and frustration rose in her, and with them came hatred for the evil girl who had caused so much horror. Aline caught hold of that hatred, and summoned all her passion in one great surge of willpower.

The scene in the mirror twisted, changed. She felt a wave of searing, incredible heat, and suddenly there was smoke in her eyes, in her nose and mouth, the smell of it, the taste of it – she had broken through.

She could feel the grip of Orielle's hand, but Orielle seemed unreal now, part of a dream. *This* was reality; this choking, churning tumult of the mirror world. The entire north wing was burning, she realized; just as the real north wing had burned two years ago. And somewhere in the midst of the havoc was Orlando.

'*Orlando!*' She screamed his name. '*Orlando!*'

Another cry answered her; not Orlando's voice but a wild shriek of rage as Zilla realized what was afoot. Suddenly there was a commotion a short way off, and two struggling figures burst out of the smoke. Orlando tried to reach Aline, but Zilla's hands were clamped like claws on his wrists. Her eyes blazed as madly as the flames and with her unhuman, unnatural power she was dragging him slowly back towards the fire. The flames roared up; Orlando and Zilla were swaying, battling silhouettes against the blaze, and with a hideous certainty Aline knew that his strength wasn't enough. There was only one hope. And if it failed, they would both die.

She took one deep breath, inhaling smoke but knowing that it was her last chance before breathing became impossible. Then she loosened her grip on Orielle, pushed her hand away, and plunged into the seething heat and darkness.

CHAPTER XI

'ORLANDO! ORLANDO!' Like the cry of a lost bird, Aline's voice rang through the uproar of the blazing wing. She could see Orlando and Zilla, and she stumbled towards them, her hands reaching out. The heat was stunning and she could feel perspiration streaming down her face. With a desperate lunge she grabbed Orlando's arm. Taken by surprise, Zilla staggered back and lost her hold on him.

'*Run!*' Aline coughed the word out. Eyes streaming, they turned and groped their way back towards the mirror. They could see it looming in the murk, and see Orielle's vague shape in the real world beyond. Another step, another; they were almost there, they could almost touch the frame – and in a final, staggering lurch they flung themselves at the doorway between the two worlds. Aline saw Orlando go through; she dived after him –

And from behind her, fingers closed like steel on her ankle.

Zilla! She had hold of Aline, and though Aline kicked furiously she couldn't break the ghost-girl's monstrous grip. She felt herself being pulled steadily, relentlessly back. She tried to hang on to the mirror's frame, but it was useless. She was losing her balance; she was falling back into the deadly world of the fire . . .

With a yell Aline let go of the mirror and pitched backwards, hitting the floor of the other world with bone-jarring force. She landed in ash and rubble; as she rolled over she saw Zilla's figure looming above here, and saw the burning brand she held. Zilla wasn't going to wait for the fire to do its work. She raised the brand high, before swinging it savagely down towards Aline's face.

Aline's scream was eclipsed by a shout of fury, and Orlando appeared from the mirror. As the brand came down, he hurled himself between Zilla and her prey. The blazing torch seared across his arm and his sleeve caught fire, but he ignored it. His hand clamped on Zilla's wrist. Shocked, she reeled under the onslaught, and in one single, ferocious movement Orlando pushed her backwards. Zilla tottered, spun around, stumbled – and with a colossal roar and an eruption of sparks, the roof of the mirror-world house caved in. In a daze Aline saw the huge, burning timbers crashing down. Then she was jerked to her feet and pulled across the floor. She heard Zilla's last, hideous shriek as the fire engulfed her, and the sound of it rose shrilly through the greater din as, with a second to spare, she and Orlando pitched back through the mirror.

Gasping, dragging clean air into her lungs,

Aline sprawled on the floor of the ruined wing. Through a dizzy haze she heard Orielle's voice; saw her beating out the flames on Orlando's sleeve. Then hands took hold of her, helping her to sit up, and suddenly Orlando was holding her tightly, crushing her to him so that she could feel his heart pounding against her.

'Aline . . .' His voice was hoarse with exhaustion, and also with emotion. 'Oh, Aline . . .'

Aline couldn't speak. There were no words she could find. Clinging to him, she stared into the mirror, into the world that had so nearly killed them both. The fire was consuming that world now. They could not see Zilla. All they could hear was the faint sound of the blaze, like a noise from a distant dream. But they all knew that, this time, the ghost-girl could not have escaped her fate. At last, Zilla was truly dead.

Slowly, Orlando released his hold on Aline. He stood up and, sombrely, took a step towards the mirror.

'This time,' he said quietly, 'we'll make no mistake. We'll make sure that the past can never come back to haunt us again.'

Aline and Orielle understood. They reached out, and they began to pull away the shards of glass. The pieces came easily – almost as if they were glad to go, Aline thought with an inward shudder – and as they were dismantled, so the glare of the fire in the other world began to fade. Faint glimmerings of light still showed in each discarded sliver, but as the very last shard was removed, the lights flared briefly and winked out. Darkness came softly down on them. And all was silent.

Gradually, their eyes adjusted to the dimness. There was a moon tonight, and its glow came in through the broken roof and windows. It wasn't strong, but it was enough for them to see each other's faces; each other's weary but thankful smiles. When Orlando took Aline into his arms and kissed her, Orielle turned tactfully away, a poignant smile on her face. And when the embrace ended she said, in a voice that shook a little, 'Whatever would our guests think if they could see us all now . . .?'

Aline and Orlando looked at her, and Orlando even managed a fragile laugh. The ball seemed a lifetime away. Then, quickly and warmly, Orlando bent to kiss his sister.

'Aline,' he said, 'help me lift Orielle back into her chair.' He paused. 'Though I'm not sure whether she'll need it for much longer.'

Orielle looked away again. But Aline knew what she was thinking. Tonight, desperation had given her the will to use her legs again. It had been a small triumph; there was no strength left in her now and she didn't yet trust that she would ever be able to do such a thing again. But she had overcome one barrier. And where one had fallen, might not others follow?

Aline reached out and took hold of Orlando's

hand. She felt as if she never wanted to let it go again. But now, there would be no more fear. Only happiness . . . for them all.

'We'll help you, Orielle,' she said very gently. 'Both of us.'

Orielle looked up at her. There was a glimmer of tears in her eyes, but after a moment she blinked them away and smiled. The past was gone. The shadow was banished.

'Yes,' she replied. Then a small hint of elation broke through her wistfulness. 'And who knows,' she added, her look suddenly warm and filled with hope, 'I might even dance at your wedding!'

About the Author

Louise Cooper was born in Hertfordshire in 1952. She hated school so much – spending most lessons clandestinely writing stories – that she persuaded her parents to let her abandon her education at the age of fifteen, and has never regretted it. Her first novel was published when she was twenty. She moved to London in 1975 and worked in publishing before becoming a full-time writer in 1977. Since then, she has published more than twenty fantasy novels for both adults and children, and has ideas for many more to come. She also writes occasional short stories, and poetry for her own pleasure.

Also in the DARK ENCHANTMENT series

Valley of Wolves
by THERESA RADCLIFFE

CHAPTER I

THE TRAVELLER URGED on his horse. He was beginning to wish he'd not left the journey so late, or rather that he hadn't made it at all. The evening was closing in with alarming speed. The heavy clouds and biting wind could mean only one thing – snow was coming. The road through the mountains was flanked on either side by dark forests of fir and spruce. Even in daylight it was a sombre, forbidding place. Now, as dusk descended, it was the last place on earth the young lawyer wanted to find himself.

He was heading for the monastery of St Cleux, which lay on a remote hillside beyond the mountains. It was not so much the abbot's urgent summons that had brought him out, but the anticipation of a handsome fee. Mysteriously untouched by the plague, this isolated monastery had prospered in recent years and could still pay well for his services. Elsewhere plague, famine and harsh winters had devastated the country, bringing poverty and starvation to many. Wolves had left the mountains and forests and come down to the valleys to ravage towns and villages, carrying off unguarded livestock and unwary children or travellers.

The lawyer came upon the carriage quite suddenly, as the road turned a bend. It lay on its side, half off the road. Only a cluster of pine trees had prevented it slipping down the steep ravine. Pulling his horse to an abrupt halt, the shocked traveller kept his seat. He was uncertain whether he'd come upon the scene of some real misfortune, or whether this was an ambush set by evil brigands. He brought his horse forward cautiously, keeping alert to any sounds or movements that might indicate a hidden assailant. But as he drew nearer, he saw the gilded lilies and ravens on the carriage door and recognized at once the crest of the de Guise family. This was undoubtedly the carriage of the Count himself. Some terrible accident must have overtaken the Count and Countess de Guise.

The wind had dropped and flakes of snow were beginning to fall. The forest was strangely silent. The only sounds the traveller could hear were his horse's laboured breathing and his own heart pounding. He gripped the reins tightly. He desperately wanted to ride on, but knew he could not. He dismounted slowly, steeling himself against what he might find, trying to suppress the inexplicable anxiety that filled him. After all, the horses had gone, and this was surely a good sign. The unfortunate occupants, unable to right the carriage, would have surely ridden off to find help rather than spend a night on this dangerous, desolate highway.

The young lawyer could see nothing from the road side of the carriage. He moved slowly round, holding on to the chassis and wheels to prevent himself slipping down the bank. The Count, he knew it was the Count by his fine boots and clothing, was lying face down some way from the carriage. A servant was stretched out in a pool of blood close by. The Countess, wrapped in furs and fine ermine, lay half in, half out of the carriage door, the wound on her neck like a ribbon of garnet against the white fur.

The lawyer stood very still, as though needing time to take in the terrible scene in front of him. Then came the first howl, long, slow and mournful, jerking him back into action, to thoughts of his own safety. Then another and another, a rising chorus echoing through the forest. Wolves! He stumbled back up the bank. His horse was already moving its head and pawing the ground in alarm. He knew he had to reach his horse before fresh howling broke out and the terrified animal took off without him.

He approached the horse slowly, whispering soothing words. He mounted. He wanted to fly, to tear down the mountain, away from this awful scene, away from the wolves. But the snow was falling steadily now and it was nearly dark. One stumble, one slip and he could be thrown. Keeping a tight rein, he set off at a careful, steady pace.

As they moved slowly down the mountain, it seemed that the forest had come alive. Shadows were sliding between the trees. He could see the glimmer, the glint of flashing eyes and lean, hungry shapes stealing through the pines, padding silently towards the carriage. Suddenly he could bear it no longer. Grasping the horse's neck and digging in his heels, the lawyer set off at full gallop down the mountainside.

Somehow, by luck and good fortune, the young lawyer did reach the monastery of St Cleux that night and still in one piece. The surprised monks took him in out of the blizzard which was now raging. The trembling and frozen traveller told them his tale.

Nothing could be done that night, but the following morning the monks and the young lawyer set out through the snow to try and recover the unfortunate Count and Countess. They were joined on the road by a search-party from a town in the next valley, where the Count and his family had been expected the previous day. It seemed that the Count de Guise had been accompanied not only by his wife, but also his young son and heir, Jean-Pierre. The boy was some ten or eleven years old. Hearing this, the lawyer was thrown into great turmoil, for he had seen no sign of any child. But then nor had he, for sudden fear of the wolves, made any search of the area. He had not even looked inside the carriage itself. Suppose the boy was trapped in there. Would he have survived the night? What would they find?

At last they reached the scene. The forest was glistening now, white and shimmering in the cold sun. Snow covered the ground, the carriage, the overhanging trees; white snow, pure and unblemished. But beyond the road the trammelled snow – red now and horribly disturbed – revealed that the wolves had been at work. Only a few bloodied rags remained. No trace was ever found of the boy. It seemed that the whole noble family of de Guise had been wiped out in a single night . . .

Also in **DARK ENCHANTMENT**

Blood Dance

by LOUISE COOPER

Garland expects her betrothal
to the man she loves to bring her
happiness. But her new life is
threatened by a dark, supernatural
power from which there seems to be
no escape – unless she can find the
answer to a long-lost secret.

Also in DARK ENCHANTMENT

Dance with the Vampire

by J. B. CALCHMAN

Ella and Alex's arrival in Oakport, Maine, stirs intense feelings. This is the place where Alex's parents died, and his Uncle Ethan is the man Alex holds responsible. Why then is Ella so strangely attracted to Ethan? And what will she do when the bond between them threatens everyone's happiness?

Also in DARK ENCHANTMENT

Firespell

by LOUISE COOPER

When Lianne looks into the heart of the topaz, she discovers the man she is to fall in love with – and at the same time reawakens an old family curse. But is the handsome face that beckons her from within the jewel one of good or evil? Is he from this world or the next? And can Lianne's love ever win?

Also in DARK ENCHANTMENT

The Hounds of Winter

by LOUISE COOPER

Tavia's marriage to a handsome but mysterious aristocrat kindles her sister Jansie's jealousy – but it also awakens a sinister force. For, as the first snow falls, the hounds of winter are unleashed and danger closes in. Can Jansie save her sister and herself?

Also in **DARK ENCHANTMENT**

House of Thorns

by JUDY DELAGHTY

When Elaine and Gwen seek their
fortunes in the gypsy camp, Elaine's
destiny is woven into a dark mystery.
Will she be forced to marry Peter,
Heir of Thorncliffe, or can she find
a magical way to escape?

READ MORE IN PUFFIN

For children of all ages, Puffin represents quality and variety – the very best in publishing today around the world.

For complete information about books available from Puffin – and Penguin – and how to order them, contact us at the appropriate address below. Please note that for copyright reasons the selection of books varies from country to country.

On the world wide web: www.penguin.co.uk

In the United Kingdom: Please write to Dept. EP, Penguin Books Ltd, Bath Road, Harmondsworth, West Drayton, Middlesex UB7 ODA

In the United States: Please write to Consumer Sales, Penguin USA, P.O. Box 999, Dept. 17109, Bergenfield, New Jersey 07621-0120. VISA and MasterCard holders call 1-800-253-6476 to order Penguin titles

In Canada: Please write to Penguin Books Canada Ltd, 10 Alcorn Avenue, Suite 300, Toronto, Ontario M4V 3B2

In Australia: Please write to Penguin Books Australia Ltd, P.O. Box 257, Ringwood, Victoria 3134

In New Zealand: Please write to Penguin Books (NZ) Ltd, Private Bag 102902, North Shore Mail Centre, Auckland 10

In India: Please write to Penguin Books India Pvt Ltd, 706 Eros Apartments, 56 Nehru Place, New Delhi 110 019

In the Netherlands: Please write to Penguin Books Netherlands bv, Postbus 3507, NL-1001 AH Amsterdam

In Germany: Please write to Penguin Books Deutschland GmbH, Metzlerstrasse 26, 60594 Frankfurt am Main

In Spain: Please write to Penguin Books S. A., Bravo Murillo 19, 1° B, 28015 Madrid

In Italy: Please write to Penguin Italia s.r.l., Via Felice Casati 20, I–20124 Milano

In France: Please write to Penguin France S. A., 17 rue Lejeune, F–31000 Toulouse

In Japan: Please write to Penguin Books Japan, Ishikiribashi Building, 2–5–4, Suido, Bunkyo-ku, Tokyo 112

In South Africa: Please write to Longman Penguin Southern Africa (Pty) Ltd, Private Bag X08, Bertsham 2013